View Finder
By Scott Duck

D1569239

Acknowledgements

Many people have helped to make this book possible. I would like to thank my wife, Lara, for her suggestions and her help in editing the manuscript. I would also like to thank Carroll Griffin and Jerry Potter for their suggestions and help in editing. I thank everyone who have offered support through encouragement, prayer, and purchasing my books. Most of all, I thank Jesus Christ, who is my Lord and Savior, Who has called me to this ministry through writing, and through Whom all things are possible.

Disclaimer

This novel is a work of fiction. The characters, names, incidents, dialogue, and plot are the products of the author's imagination or are used fictitiously. Any resemblance to actual persons or events is purely coincidental.

Chapter 1

October 2014.

Christine Richardson slowly rolled over and reached out for her iPhone. She looked at the time. It was 6:08 am. That was good. She had slept a full eight hours, which had become very unusual lately. She had been having trouble sleeping since not long after she had gotten pregnant, six months ago. She rolled onto her back and looked up at the ceiling. Actually, she felt pretty good this morning. No morning sickness. Not much pain in her back and hips, which had been a problem lately. She decided to go ahead and get the day started. She rose carefully, so as not to wake Dan, and tiptoed out of the bedroom.

On her way to the kitchen, she stopped by the bathroom. She couldn't pass it without stopping lately. She couldn't pass the nursery without stopping either and she now stood in the door, surveying the room. She and Dan had done it in the last month or so. Actually, she had picked everything out and Dan had done all of the work. He wouldn't let her do anything since getting pregnant, especially as she had approached the third trimester. She looked at the crib and the bedding that it had taken her six weeks to pick out. She looked at the animals on the walls that she herself had drawn and Dan had painted. She looked at the scripture on the wall above the crib. She felt a longing to hold this little life that she hadn't even met yet but who God knew even from before the foundation of the world.

When she got to the kitchen, she started the coffee and poured herself a bowl of cereal. As she ate, she thought about her life and how it had changed in the past year. She had married Dan almost one year ago. What a year it had been.

Things had started out a bit rough, partly because of his initial reluctance to get involved in church, but when things had changed in that regard, they really changed. Now, not only did he attend every service but he also got up early every morning to spend time in prayer and bible study. He had even begun frequently helping out around the church and had started talking about perhaps someday teaching a Sunday school or discipleship class. She smiled as she thought back to the Sunday afternoon, six months previously, when he had been so excited that he had almost knocked her down as he literally ran into the room to tell her of his salvation experience. Her reverie was interrupted by the thump of the newspaper against the front door.

She got up and went to the front door, pausing for a moment to place her hand flat on the biometric reader just to the right of the door. In less than a second, she heard a soft beep, which indicated that the intrusion alarm was deactivated for this particular door, followed by the slight clicking sound of the electronic lock being released. This was all part of the very elaborate security system that Dan had installed before they even moved into the house. Not only was there the security system but there was a man on guard every evening, from 10:00pm until 6:00am. All this security sometimes made Christine feel like she was living in a prison but she understood that it was necessary. Dan had made some dangerous enemies in the world of organized crime when he had uncovered a money laundering operation which involved Vision Biotech, a company which had brought eye site to Dan's previously blind brother, Jake, and a company which Dan now owned.

When she opened the door to get the paper, she noticed what a beautiful morning it was, and she decided to take her coffee and the paper out onto the back deck and sit for a while. She went through the same routine with the security system at the back door and she took the paper to the table and spread it out. She smiled when she saw the front page article, titled "Second Man to Receive Miracle of Sight From Local Biotech

2

Company". The company that the article referred to was Vision Biotech and the man who was to soon receive his eye sight was David Landers, a famous blind Christian musical composer and performer. Dan's brother, Jake, had been the first to receive eye sight through the technology that had been developed by the company. It was Jake who convinced David to go through with the procedure. Jake and David had talked a lot about Jake's own experience and David was very excited. His own procedure was to occur in about a week.

While she was sitting there, she noticed a small object on the ground, just a few feet away from the deck. It was small and rectangular, about the size of a pack of cigarettes. At first, she thought little of it and she just kept drinking her coffee and reading her paper. Out of the corner of her eye, she occasionally noticed a little flash of light from the object. At first, she thought that it was sunlight glinting off of it. But, no, that couldn't be it because she was staring straight at it now and the light was coming in very regular intervals. And the object was white but was the light green? Yes, it was. This definitely was not reflected sun light. Her curiosity was peeked and she decided to investigate.

She got up and carefully went down the deck steps. She certainly didn't want to fall at this point in her pregnancy. She bent over the object. It was about the size of a iPhone, but a bit thicker, solid white, with a little blinking green light on one end. Suddenly, she heard a noise behind her. Just as she started to straighten up, she felt a crashing blow to the back of her head. She managed to turn as she fell, to avoid falling on her stomach and hurting the baby, she hoped. As she hit the ground, the world swam out of focus for a moment and she thought that she would pass out. When things came back in focus, she wished that she had passed out. She stared up in disbelief at the person standing over her.

"Jake!"

Chapter 2

Eight months earlier, February 2014.

"That sure is a whole lot of money."

"Yes, it is, but take it from me, it will be worth it."

David Landers and Jake Richardson sat discussing the possibility of David becoming one of Vision Biotech's gold patients. There would be only three gold patients. They would be among the first blind people to receive eyesight through the technology that had been developed by Vision Biotech. In exchange for the privilege of reaping the benefits of the technology far sooner than anyone else, they would pay a premium for the procedure, ten million dollars, as opposed to the approximately half a million that would be paid by future patients or, in most cases, paid by their insurers. Jake had been the very first to receive eyesight through this technology and he was also the brother of the man who now owned the company. As such, he was the perfect choice to head up the effort to recruit the gold patients. David was his first attempt and he was proving to be a tougher sale than Jake had expected.

"Well Jake, take a second to look at this from my prospective. It is awesome that you went from complete blindness to completely normal vision. I can't even imagine how that would feel. I would love to find out and I would give almost anything to do just that. No doubt, it is worth a lot, a whole lot, but I'm not sure it is worth ten million dollars. I have made a lot of money in my career but even I can't just write a check for ten million dollars. I could come up with the money but, as I said, I don't know that it's worth that much. I know that you think that it is worth that but you didn't pay that much, did you?"

Jake wondered if this was how David really felt or if this was just part of his negotiating tactics. Jake would have given just about anything that he had to give for his eyesight. In reality though, Jake hadn't had much money and it had been only Dan's generosity that had made it possible for Jake to receive his sight.

"Well, no, I didn't."

"How much did you pay?"

Dan had not actually paid anything directly for the procedure but he had kept the company afloat long enough for the procedure to be done. In total, Dan had sunk about three million dollars into the company. Jake was a little ashamed that he had not been successful enough to have anything to personally contribute financially. When he answered, he hedged a little.

"About three million was paid."

"About three million. And you want me to pay ten million?"

"Well, it's sort of complicated. It wasn't my money, it was my brother Dan's money. He was the CFO at the time. Also, it wasn't actually a fee for the procedure, it was used in order to insure the company's survival long enough for the procedure to be performed and, in exchange for providing the needed capital, Dan received a 10% stake in the company."

It bothered Jake having to tell David about the details surrounding Jake's own procedure. For one thing, he wasn't entirely sure that it was any of David's business. For another thing, telling David the details meant having to admit that Jake, himself, had contributed nothing. Sure, Jake had had a hard time with employment because of his blindness but would David understand that? After all, David was himself blind, yet he had made millions. Would he see Jake as someone who leaned on his blindness as a crutch, lazily living on the generosity of others? Or had David also faced financial struggles related to his blindness before he had made it big? Jake watched David for some indication of what he thought of Jake's revelations but he could discern nothing from his body language or facial expressions.

After appearing to ponder what Jake had said for a few seconds, David spoke.

"I see. Well, that does make your situation with the three million a little different. I am still unclear on some of the details. How did Dan end up going from CFO to CEO?"

"I'm sure that you saw everything in the press concerning the connection between Ben Nelson, who was the founder of Vision Biotech, and the mob money laundering operation."

David nodded.

"And you also saw the press coverage concerning the attempt to injure or kill me by sabotaging my implants?"

David nodded again.

"Well, with all of that negative press, Ben couldn't possibly attract any more investors. Thinking that it was better to get a little something for all his work, he sold his remaining 90% of the company to Dan for very little. Dan then planned to get some venture capital to revitalize the company and continue the work that Vision Biotech had already started. After all, I'm proof that the technology works. But attracting venture capital has proven more difficult than Dan had thought. There are a couple other investors but they don't have the kind of money that it will take to get the company off the ground again. That's why the gold patients are so important and that's why we are charging them ten million dollars each."

David pondered that for a long moment.

"Hmmm. That does shed a bit of a different light on things but I'm still not sure. Give me a few days to think about it and I'll get back to you."

"Sure. Take your time."

As David got his cane and made his way out to the car where his driver was waiting, Jake thought over the conversation that they had just had. Jake did not like having had to go into so much detail but he was cautiously optimistic that it would be enough to convince David to become a gold patient. He headed to Dan's office to talk to him about the meeting.

7

Chapter 3

When Jake walked into Dan's office, his desk was covered with several binders and stacks of papers. Dan sat staring at his computer screen, deep in thought, and Jake took a seat and waited. Jake thought that Dan looked a little worried and, after several minutes without being acknowledged, Jake slapped his hand on the desk. Dan jumped.

"Crap! Don't do that!"

"At least I got you to acknowledge my presence."

"Sorry. I'm a little preoccupied."

"I can see that. What are you doing?"

"I'm looking at our capital requirements to get this thing off the ground.

"How are things looking?"

"Our biggest short term cash expenditure is going to be with Biotronics."

"The company who manufactured my artificial retinal implants, after Vision Biotech designed them."

"That's right. They are also going to manufacture the implants for the gold patients. They are the most logical choice because they have the only people on the planet, other than Ben, who are familiar with the inner workings of the technology so they can do it faster than anybody else."

"That's great. I'm sure they could do it even faster if they still had James Swanson working there."

James Swanson had been the head laboratory technician at Biotronics until James had taken part in a plan to sabotage Jake's implants. James, himself, had no apparent motive and so it was assumed that he had been paid to do it but no one had ever found out who had hired him. He was currently serving a ten year jail sentence for it.

"Yeah, I'm sure things would be much faster and much smoother with James' help. No chance of that though. Not with him sitting in a jail cell."

"Yeah and, anyway, I'm not sure I would want him working on it, not with what he tried to do to me."

"I agree. I really hate it for his wife and kids though. She seems like a good person and things are going to be really hard for them now."

Just then, Dan's phone rang and Jake excused himself to get started working on finding and recruiting the next gold patient.

Chapter 4

As Jake left, Dan looked at the caller ID on his iPhone. It showed that Mike Hannon was calling. Dan was pleased. Mike had been something of a mentor to Dan in Dan's college and early career days. Mike had also conducted the valuation of R and R Accounting, in Atlanta, when Dan had recently sold out his portion to his partners and moved back to Jackson, Tennessee. Now, Dan needed Mike's help with something else and had been playing phone tag with him for a couple days.

"Hey Mike. How's it going?"

"Going great! Glad I finally caught you. What's going on in your world? How's married life treating you?"

"Oh, it's great. Absolutely terrific. Christine is a wonderful woman. We're even already starting to talk about having children. She's almost perfect. She would be perfect, if only I could get her to quit nagging me about church. I'm sure that will stop eventually though."

"Oh, what's so bad about church?"

"Well, nothing I guess. I just spend so many hours working. Then, in what little time I do have off, I would like to relax."

"Well, relax at church then."

"Church isn't relaxing. It's full of people who think they're better than you and a preacher who tells you how to live and tries to get your money."

"Hmmm. A pretty cynical perspective."

"You don't agree?"

"Well, no, I don't. As a matter of fact, I'm headed to church as soon as I hang up."

"Oh yeah, it is Wednesday isn't it? Crap. Christine will want me to go tonight. She really liked the pastor who did our wedding and she has started going to his church. Not every time the doors are open but a lot. Too often for my taste, especially if she expects me to go."

Mike paused for a moment.

"Well, anyway, what can I do for you?"

Dan noticed Mike's hesitation and abrupt change of subject. He wondered if he had offended him. What was it with these people and church? First Christine and now Mike. Gee whiz! Oh well.

"I need you to do a formal evaluation of the company's financial condition and likely future financial performance. We are recruiting what we call gold patients, in order to try to raise enough capital to get this thing off of the ground, but I'm not sure it is going to be enough. I want to get things ready to ask the bank for a loan and, of course, they will want to see an evaluation like this."

They talked for a few more minutes, with Mike asking questions and Dan explaining the situation in more detail. The conversation ended with them agreeing to have lunch the next day to discuss things further.

As Dan hung up, he was thinking about church and how he didn't want to go. He decided that he would work late. He did have a lot to do and that would solve the church problem too, for tonight anyway. Before he had even put the phone down, he called Christine to tell her.

Chapter 5

Ben Nelson sat in the dark and thought about what his life had become.

Just four months previously, he had been one of the most accomplished scientists of the modern age and he had been on the verge of being one of the most revered too. Limitless respect, power, and wealth were within his grasp. Then, it had all come crashing down.

Ben was the founder of Vision Biotech, the company which had developed what promised to be a cure for blindness in tens of thousands of people. In his pursuit of this goal, Ben's overzealousness and lust for power and money had led him to get mixed up with the Patrillo crime family. Eventually, Ben's connection to the crime family had been revealed when Vinnie Patrillo, the head of the crime family, had Jake and Christine kidnapped in an attempt to keep them from revealing what they and Dan had learned about the Patrillos providing funding to the company. Though Ben had not known that the kidnapping would occur, the incident generated a lot of bad press and Ben feared prosecution. In disgrace, he had offered to sell Dan the company for $500,000, less than he felt it was worth but more than he was likely to get anywhere else. Dan had accepted Ben's offer and with Ben's 90% together with the 10% that Dan already owned, Dan was now the sole owner of the company.

Ben thought about that on this sleepless night as he sat in his living room, at 3:00am, with the lights off, staring straight ahead and seeing nothing but the darkness. He thought that it was quite ironic that, just as the technology that he had created was poised to bring light to the world of thousands, utter darkness had descended on his world, deeper than the darkness in this room. He had lost his company. He had lost his respect in the scientific community. He had lost his prospect for future wealth. He had lost Cathy. He had lost everything that meant anything to him. But he wasn't finished yet. He was a man of planning and action. That was one of the things that had taken him so far before his fall. Through all the sleepless nights that he had recently endured, he had formulated a plan.

He reached out in the darkness and felt for the switch on the lamp beside his chair. As he twisted it and the light stung his eyes, he spoke aloud.

"Just as this light chases the shadows from this room, the technology that I created will yet chase the shadows from my world, just as, in a different way, it will chase the darkness from the worlds of countless others. I, not the Richardsons, will be there to rightfully reap the benefits of my creation."

First thing first though. He had to put his plan into action and, in order to do that, he had to get a job working for Vision Biotech.

Chapter 6

Thursday morning, Dan sat back in his chair and rubbed his eyes. He was getting a headache. He needed some ibuprofen and some coffee. He was still going over the capital requirement numbers and he did not like what he was seeing. He decided to take a break for a while and go get that coffee and ibuprofen.

Dan was still in the same building that he had rented when he had needed office space in Jackson in order to remotely perform the function of chief financial officer for Vision Biotech which had been, at that time, based in Memphis. As he made his way to the kitchen, Dan thought about the fact that they were going to need more space. The owner of the building had recently offered to sell the building at a very good price, when he had learned that Dan had purchased Vision Biotech and had set up the company's headquarters there. Dan liked the place and would like to have bought it and expanded it but, with the way that things were looking financially, that was going to have to wait for a while. As he started to make the coffee, he sighed as he made a mental note to write the rent check for the month.

As the coffee was brewing, Jake came in and sat down in one of two chairs at the small table in the corner. Dan collapsed heavily into the other chair as he breathed an exasperated "good morning". Jake returned the greeting and, after a brief pause, he spoke.

"You look worried. Don't get me wrong, it's pretty cool to be able to tell how you look, but if you are worried then I probably need to be worried too. I can't stand sleeping well and being relatively care free when I should be stressed to the max. What's up?"

Dan laughed in spite of himself.

"Well, I'm just a little worried about the finances around here."

"Really?"

"Yeah. I've been looking at the amount of money that we're going to need to get this thing off the ground and I'm getting a little worried that we're not going to be able to come up with it."

Now Jake had a worried look on his face too. They sat in silence for a few seconds before Dan spoke again.

"How did things go with David Landers yesterday? I never got a chance to ask."

"He's going to be a harder sell than I thought. In a nutshell, he just isn't sure it's worth the price."

"Really? I would have thought that he would consider any price a bargain."

"You would think. Then again, he hasn't had much trouble managing so far. I mean, he has been extraordinarily successful, despite his blindness. It appears that his blindness has not hampered him as much as mine did, at least from a monetary prospective, and so he may not be quite as anxious to receive his sight as I was."

Dan sat in thought for a moment.

"Putting the financial matters aside for a moment, do I detect a note of insecurity concerning your own accomplishments when you were blind?"

"Well, you have to admit, I didn't accomplish that much."

"The heck you didn't! You did very well in school and went on to get a college degree, which is something that a lot of sighted people don't do. Then, you supported yourself well, for years."

"Yes, I supported myself well for years and now I haven't supported myself at all for quite a while, at least until now, and even now it is you who gave me this job. Even before this job, for the last couple years, I would not have survived financially, were it not for you. So, no, I don't think I accomplished much as a blind man. Now, can we get back to the financial issues?"

Dan was disturbed by what Jake had said and by his defensive tone but he didn't really know what else to say on the subject at the moment. After a moment of awkward silence, Dan spoke.

"OK, sure, we can get back to business. Our biggest capital problem is going to be with Biotronics, which I eluded to a bit yesterday. After the mess that Ben got into with this company, Biotronics thought they were finished because they had been struggling for years and Vision Biotech had been the only thing keeping them afloat. They sold all their equipment, at a significant loss, and used the money to pay their considerable debt. So, we are going to have to provide them with enough capital to completely reequip. We will get that initial investment back in the form of lower prices from them later, when they are manufacturing all our implants, but that's later. Right now, we have to come up with the money and our prospects for getting it are looking less likely than I had expected."

Jake whistled.

"Wow. They are going to have to completely reequip? Man, that's not good."

"No, it isn't good. One thing that will make the equipment much more expensive is that we don't have some critical information concerning the design of the implants. So, they are going to have to get some equipment that can be used to reverse engineer some things, using one of your implants as a reference."

Dan waited for a reaction. He didn't have to wait long.

Jake shouted.

"What! Reengineer? From one of my implants? No!"

"Jake, listen."

"I'm not listening to anything! I won't do it!"

"But it's the only way."

Jake was no longer shouting but he had an edge to his voice.

17

"Well, we will have to find another way. I have finally got vision as good as yours. I'm not taking a chance on losing it. In order to reengineer anything, they would have to remove the implant. If they do that, there's no guarantee that something won't happen to it or that there won't be problems putting it back in. I simply will not do it. That's final. End of discussion."

Jake looked very angry and a bit panicked as he got up and stormed out.

Dan sighed and placed his head in his hands. He had expected some possible opposition but not the extreme anger and panicked reaction that he had gotten. Now what was he going to do?

Chapter 7

Jake sat in his office and silently fumed. There were so many emotions coursing through him. He was embarrassed at having acted toward Dan in the way that he had. He was angry that Dan wanted to remove one of his implants, even temporarily, so that he could reverse engineer it. He was scared at the thought that he might end up going along with Dan's plan and then something could go wrong and he would then end up losing his newly acquired vision. Mostly, he was angry with himself for feeling so out of control at the mere mention of something being done to his implants.

He got up and paced. He wanted to leave the building. He knew that Dan might come and want to talk to him and he didn't want that, not right now. He wished that he could go for a drive. He had a brand new truck that Dan had bought for him, sitting in his garage, just waiting for him to get behind the wheel, but with everything that had been going on lately, he had not made getting his license a priority. He thought about the shiny black Chevrolet Silverado and he now regretted his lack of diligence in getting his license and that just added to his mounting frustration.

He knew that it wasn't good that he felt this sudden extreme protective reaction concerning his vision. It was causing him to act not at all like himself and he hated the feelings that it evoked but what should he do about it? What could he do? His frustration mounted and his mood darkened as he continued to pace.

Suddenly, there was a knock at Jake's office door. What!"

Dan opened the door and stuck his head in. Jake stopped his pacing and glared at Dan. Dan appeared not to notice.

"I just wanted to let you know that I'm headed out to have lunch with Mike."

"OK, thanks."

"You want to come?"

"No thanks."

"You want me to bring you something back?"

"No thank you. I'm not hungry."

"OK. If you change your mind, call me."

"OK, I will."

There was an uncomfortable pause before Dan spoke again.

"Listen, Jake, about what we were talking about earlier."

"Dan! I don't want to talk about it! Not right now. OK?"

Dan looked hurt.

"OK."

Dan closed the door and left.

Jake collapsed into his chair. What was wrong with him? He didn't know but he knew that he had to calm down and get a handle on this.

Chapter 8

Mike Hannon sat in the parking lot of Logan's restaurant, waiting for Dan to arrive for their scheduled lunch meeting. As Mike waited, he thought back to the phone conversation with Dan the previous afternoon.

He just didn't understand Dan's very cynical attitude about Christianity. It didn't really seem to fit with Dan's overall character and personality. Mike knew that part of the problem was that Dan didn't really understand Christianity. What was it Dan had said yesterday? "Church is full of people who think they're better than you and a preacher who tells you how to live and tries to get your money." Mike had to admit to himself that a perspective like that was understandable for someone who hadn't grown up in church, as Mike had. He also had to admit to himself that he hadn't helped Dan's prospective of Christianity in that he hadn't tried very hard to change that prospective, a fact of which he was deeply ashamed.

He thought back to the conversation that he and Dan had over lunch, back in Atlanta, about a year previously, when they had been working on a valuation of R and R Accounting. That had also been a very good opportunity to witness to Dan. Dan had basically said that he thought that Christianity was about studying the bible and trying to be a good person. Then as now, Mike had blown that opportunity to share his faith and what it meant to him, to share the Gospel message of how Dan too could have the joy and peace in Christ that Mike had. Mike didn't feel very at peace right now. He hoped that he would have yet another opportunity to share his faith with Dan but he feared failing yet again when presented with such an opportunity. As these feelings of inadequacy washed over him, he began to pray.

"Lord. I thank you for your grace that is abundantly and freely given. I want to apologize that I have done such a poor job of telling people about You. You have done so much for me. I should tell people how they can have the same relationship with you that I have and I want to do that Lord but, when it comes to sharing my faith, I am so timid. Please Lord, help me to change that. Please start with Dan. Please give me an opportunity to talk to him about You and please give me the strength to take advantage of that opportunity. Please give me the right words to say."

As he prayed, he began to feel better about the situation. He was still ashamed at not having done a better job of sharing his faith previously and he was still a little nervous at the thought of talking to Dan about it but he knew that he had been forgiven for his previous shortcomings and he knew that God would give him strength and guidance.

As he opened his eyes and looked up after praying, he saw Dan pull into the parking lot. He saw the recognition on Dan's face when he spotted Mike's car. "Lord, here we go" Mike thought as he got out of his car.

They met up near the front door and shook hands. Dan appeared to be genuinely happy to see Mike but he also looked troubled. Mike wondered what was bothering his old friend. He hoped that it wasn't the conversation about church the previous afternoon. As soon as he had the thought, he silently criticized himself for it. There was that spiritual timidity rearing its ugly head already. "I have got to stop this" he thought, "I have got to stop worrying so much about what people think about my faith or about me discussing it". He sent up a quick and silent prayer for God to help him.

During the short wait for a table, their conversation centered around Dan's recent marriage to Christine, the new house, and a relatively superficial discussion about Dan's taking over Vision Biotech. Overall, Dan appeared to be happy but the feeling that something was troubling him persisted and

22

needled at Mike's consciousness. Perhaps it was simply the financial difficulties that Dan had mentioned the day before. Mike hoped that was the problem. Solving problems like that was something that Mike was good at. For that matter, so was Dan, which is why he had previously been able to help to build one of the most successful accounting firms in Atlanta. Mike was quite confident that they would be able to put their heads together and come up with a plan to solve whatever financial problems the company might be having and he was anxious for the conversation to move in that direction, onto solid ground where he felt comfortable.

When they sat down and ordered, Mike ordered a steak and baked potato with salad. Dan, whom Mike had always known to be a big eater, ordered only a sandwich, yet more evidence that he was troubled by something.

Soon, the conversation did turn to Vision Biotech and its financial problems.

"I knew that getting this thing going wouldn't be easy, an undertaking of this size never is, but it is turning out to be more difficult than I had anticipated."

"Oh really?"

"Yes, much more difficult."

"Well, tell me about it. From our conversation yesterday, I gather that you are having capital problems?"

"Yes. It is going to take at least twenty-five million to get us to the point of actually starting to perform the implant procedures. Once we get to that point, I don't think we will have any trouble going forward. After all, we are talking about one of the holy grails of medicine, a cure for blindness. Once it has been done another time or two and we prove that we can repeat our initial success, I think that we will have money coming in by the truck load. It is starting to look like getting to that point may be a problem though."

"Twenty five million? Why so much. I mean, the procedure has already been done once. Technologically speaking, isn't the foundation already laid?"

"Well, yes and no. For one thing, the company who manufactured the prototype implants, Biotronics, was in financial trouble and, when Vision Biotech was not able to go forward immediately, Biotronics almost folded and had to sell much of their equipment. Much of that equipment will have to be replaced. Now then, it is true that the technology has been developed and proven. As you say, this has already been done once. However, in that case, the implants were developed and manufactured over a period of years. If we are to have a viable business model, we have got to be able to manufacture these things on mass and much more quickly. That will mean purchasing and, in some cases creating, new equipment. We also have to have people to run the equipment. That won't be cheap."

Mike nodded.

"I see. Well, yesterday, you mentioned some gold patients. Tell me about those."

Dan told him about the concept they had come up with of using gold patients to raise needed capital and the problems that they had run into.

"For one thing, there just aren't many totally blind people with millions of dollars to spend on something like this. Dave Landers does have the money, or at least he can get it, but he doesn't seem as anxious as we thought to jump at the chance we are offering. He would like to have eyesight but he also seems pretty content to remain blind, if necessary."

"David Landers, the blind Christian artist and composer?"

"That's him."

"Pretty cool. I would like to meet him. Maybe I can just happen to drop by one day when he is going to be there."

"Yeah, sure. His music isn't my thing but to each his own."

"My church had him in concert last year but I wasn't able to go."

Dan nodded and they sat in silence for a moment before Dan spoke.

"Listen, Mike, about what we were talking about yesterday, about church."

Mike's pulse quickened a bit. Maybe this would be his chance and it was even Dan bringing the subject up.

"Yes?"

"I realize that I may have come on a bit strong concerning my negative feelings about church. You caught me at the end of a long and stressful day. Church isn't my thing but I don't feel as negatively about it as I may have made it appear. Besides, I do recognize that your faith is very important to you. I didn't mean to belittle that. I'm sorry."

Mike was a little excited and a little nervous. This was the perfect opportunity. Now, if he just wouldn't mess it up. He silently prayed before he answered. He had no idea what he was going to say before the words started coming out.

"That's OK Dan. No hard feelings. I do want to tell you something though. I think I can offer you a little insight as to why David Landers doesn't feel that gaining his eyesight is as important as you think it should be."

Dan started to speak and Mike held up a hand to stop him.

"Just hear me out for a second. I know David Landers to be a Christian. I have seen his Christian testimony on YouTube. He is a man of strong faith, faith in Jesus Christ. He understands that there are things much more important than the things of this world, like whether he can see or not. He probably knows that it may not be God's will that he ever see and he is probably at peace with that. In fact, I have heard him say that, in his testimony."

Dan started to speak again and Mike again stopped him.

"Hang on just one more second. You too can have that peace that I'm talking about. I have that peace. I won't bug you

25

about it but, if you are ever curious, I would love to talk to you about how to get it yourself.

Now that Mike was finally finished speaking, Dan didn't immediately try to talk. Rather than making Mike uncomfortable, as it might have done a day earlier, he used the moment of silence to thank God for the words that he had just said to Dan as he knew that they surely had not come from him. Mike knew that Dan's silence was, at least in part, shock at having never heard his longtime friend talk like this. Mike was not pleased with himself that he was just now getting around to it but he was a little proud that he finally had done it and that, with God's help, he hadn't done too badly. Now, how would Dan respond?

Dan breathed a sigh.

"Look Mike, I'm not going to pretend that I am interested right now but, you never know, one of these days, I just might be." Mike was a little disappointed at Dan's continuing lack of interest but he did count this as a small victory. At least maybe he had planted a seed that would later grow.

They moved on and talked about various methods of obtaining the financing that the company would need. By the time they were done, Dan appeared to feel much better about the financial outlook. They parted with Mike promising to call within the next couple days, after looking into a few things.

Chapter 9

As Dan drove back to the office after his lunch meeting with Mike, he thought back to their conversation. Mike had made him feel better about the company's financial future. In truth, Dan should have thought of most of the financing solutions that Mike came up with. After all, Dan's accounting and finance credentials were at least as impressive as Mike's. However, Mike was able to provide a fresh and unbiased prospective, something that was often very helpful. Dan couldn't count the number of times that he himself had pointed out solutions that were right in front of a client's face but they couldn't see it because they were too personally involved. This prompted a bit of nostalgia for his R and R days, back in Atlanta.

His thoughts then drifted to what Mike had said about Christianity. He just didn't understand why Mike and those like him got so wrapped up in all that church stuff. Mike was one of the last people that Dan would have expected to be so spiritual. Like Dan, Mike was a very pragmatic and logical person. Accounting people tended to be like that. Even so, Mike's faith appeared to bring him great comfort. Dan had intentionally not discussed Jake and the situation that had just arisen regarding the reverse engineering of his implants. Dan figured that, the way things were going, Mike would just try to spiritualize that too and Dan just didn't want to hear it right now. However, though he would barely admit it, even to himself, he was beginning to get a little curious about this personal relationship with Christ that Mike and Christine talked about.

As Dan pulled into the parking lot of Vision Biotech, he was jolted out of his reverie. Ben Nelson was sitting on the bench by the front door reading a newspaper. Dan shook his head in dismay. Just when he had begun to feel better about things!

He couldn't imagine what Ben wanted but he certainly couldn't imagine that it would be anything that he would want to hear. Just as Dan had pulled into the parking lot, a light snow had begun to fall. As he got out of his truck, he couldn't help but feel that the chill that he felt was more than just the low temperature.

Despite his misgivings about what Ben's sudden appearance might mean, Dan pasted on a smile that he hoped looked more genuine than it felt and extended his hand in greeting. Ben spoke first.

"Hey Dan! How's it going?"

"Oh, it's going fine. How are things in your world?"

At that, a flicker of unpleasantness crossed Ben's features, there and gone in an instant.

"Oh, things are going pretty well for me also. Just sort of taking my time, looking at my options."

Dan couldn't imagine that Ben really had very many options at this point.

"Really?"

"Yeah."

"You still living in Memphis?"

"Yeah, for now. I'm just in Jackson on a little business."

Dan wondered what business that might be and he feared that he was about to find out.

"So, how is married life treating you? How is Christine?"

Dan bristled at the mention of Christine. He didn't like Ben bringing her up. Although Ben supposedly did not know about the kidnapping of Christine and Jake, just over three months previously, Dan couldn't help but wonder if that was really so. Regardless of whether Ben knew about it, it was certainly Ben's involvement with the Patrillo crime family that had led to their kidnapping and it could have easily led to their death. Dan harbored few positive feelings for Ben Nelson but he tried to keep his expression positive or at least neutral.

"Oh, things are great. Christine is a wonderful woman."
Ben knew Christine well. She had been the receptionist and
secretary at Vision Biotech, when Ben still owned the
company. That was where she and Dan had met and where
she and Dan had eventually hatched a plot to get to the
bottom of some suspicious financing activity, which ultimately
exposed the connection between Ben and the Patrillos.
"Yes, she is pretty wonderful, isn't she?"
Ben's words sounded a bit forced.
"Well Ben, I'm freezing out here."
"Oh yes. Me too. Hey, could I come in and talk to you for a
few minutes?"
"Uh, yeah, sure."
Dan thought "oh great" as he unlocked the door. As he
stepped inside, he called out "Hey Jake, I'm back".
"Oh, Jake is here?"
At the mention of Jakes name, Dan bristled again. He thought
to himself "Just hold on old boy and get hold of yourself, at
least until you find out what the man wants".
"Yeah, Jake is helping me with some things. There's a whole
lot involved in getting this thing going, as you know. For
now, we are managing with just me and Jake. That will have
to change shortly though."
Dan settled in behind his desk and Ben sat across from him.
"Well, Dan, that's what I want to talk to you about."
Dan was confused.
"I don't understand. You want to talk to me about what?"
"About adding another person to your team."
For just a second, Dan was still confused. Then he got it.
"You want to come work for me?"
Dan was stunned and not in a good way. Apparently it
showed on his face or in his voice or both because Ben
immediately held up a hand in a calming gesture.
"Now hold on just a second. Let me explain."
"OK. You do that."

29

"A few minutes ago, I said that I am exploring my options. In truth, I have few options."

"I sort of figured that but I didn't want to say it."

"Of course, and I appreciate that, but I may as well be up front with you. While I am on that subject, I have always been up front with you. I really didn't know about the plot to kidnap Christine and Jake."

Dan nodded but said nothing. After a slight pause, Ben continued.

"Anyway, as I said, my options are rather limited at the moment. At the same time, you need expertise regarding the implants that I designed and I suspect that your available financial resources are rather limited at the moment, at least limited relative to what you really need."

Dan knew where Ben had to be going with this and, in spite of himself, he couldn't help but like the idea, at least a little, given the capital problems and the issues surrounding the reverse engineering of Jake's implants. As its designer, Ben knew more about this technology than anyone. If Ben were to come onboard, could that reverse engineering be unnecessary? Ben continued.

"The way I see it, I could come to work for you and offer you expertise that you could get nowhere else at a fraction of the cost that you could get inferior knowledge elsewhere. At the same time, I would be getting back into the biotech game, which is where I want to be, through the only option that I have for that right now."

"It remains to be seen whether you do, in fact, have that option. You can't just assume that we will jump at the chance. Regardless of whether you knew about what the Patrillos were going to do with Christine and Jake, we all did go through a great deal because of your connection to that crime family."

"Yes, you did, and I do sincerely apologize for that, but I can't change it now. However, I can offer you this opportunity, an opportunity for both of us. Perhaps, in a small way, this could even serve to help to make things right between us. Even if you don't care about that, which you probably don't, you have to admit that what I am offering does present you with the best chance of success. You are one of the best business men I have ever seen. Surely, you can't ignore an opportunity like this."

Dan very much doubted the sincerity of Ben's remorse and his flattery. Still, though Dan hated to admit it, he was correct. What Ben was offering did present the best chance for success. Dan couldn't just ignore that but he did need to proceed carefully.

After a moment of silent reflection, Dan spoke.

"You are right, I can't just ignore what you are offering. Neither can I just go blindly forward with it, pardon the pun. I need to do some serious thinking about this and, of course, I need to talk to Christine and Jake. Give me a few days."

"Of course."

As the men parted, Dan was in a great deal of turmoil concerning the discussion that he had just had and he couldn't wait to discuss the situation with Christine. For all her kindness, she had a way of cutting through all the bull crap and getting right to the heart of a matter. He feared that she would try to spiritualize this. No, he didn't fear it, he was certain of it. Though he had become a little curious about Christianity, he didn't want to learn about it in the midst of such a decision as this. Oh well. He didn't want to talk about this on the phone. He would rather discuss it in person and so he decided to wait until tonight to raise the issue with her. With the mood that Jake had been in this morning, Dan didn't think he wanted to throw something like this at him right now either. As he thought about that, Dan shook his head. No, that wouldn't do at all.

He would just do some serious thinking about the situation this afternoon while trying to concentrate enough to get some work done, and he would discuss it with Christine tonight.

31

Chapter 10

Christine sat in her and Dan's new home, reflecting on her life and how it had changed in the last few months. She thought back to the day she and Dan had met, when Dan had brought Jake to Vision Biotech to look into the possibility of Jake being a candidate for the technology that the company was developing. Jake had, in fact, been the first clinical trial patient, which had not only led to him gaining his eyesight but had also led to her and Dan developing a relationship which had eventually led to their marriage, just six months later. That first meeting had been the previous April. On that day, in early spring, she had been living alone, with no romantic relationships and the prospect of none, while dealing with psychological and physical harassment from her ex-husband, Roger. Now, ten months later and three months into her new marriage, she sat here, on a cold and snowy February afternoon, feeling safe and secure in her warm home, mesmerized by the flames that she saw dancing in the fireplace.

As she sat staring into the flames, she thought about Dan and how absolutely wonderful he was. He was so generous, so respectful of his parents, so supportive of Jake, so loving and patient with her. She loved him so much.

There was something that kept her from enjoying her relationship with Dan as much as she might have and that was the shadow that Roger had cast over her life. The light of Dan's love had done a lot to dispel that shadow but it was still there, making her feel unworthy of Dan's love and, despite all evidence to the contrary, making her feel, just a little bit, in the back of her mind, that Dan could turn out to be like Roger. In her interaction with Dan, she found herself seeking evidence of some hidden dark nature in him. There would sometimes be some word spoken, to her ear, a little too harshly.

Occasionally, there would be an innocent comment that she would perceive as a veiled criticism. Her feelings would be hurt. Occasionally, she would lash out but, most often, she would withdraw into herself. The change in her mood was usually subtle but Dan would still notice. As a result, she felt that he had begun to sometimes tiptoe on egg shells around her and she didn't want that. As close as they still were, she could sense them starting to drift apart a little bit, and after only three months of marriage. She feared that, if she didn't get a handle on her feelings, it would only get worse. She hated that and, deep down, she hated Roger for casting this shadow which had extended beyond herself to cover her marriage as well and keep it from being all that it could be. Still, all in all, her marriage to Dan was very good and she loved him with all her heart. As she reflected, she began to get very drowsy. The warmth of the fire and the mesmerizing sight of the dancing flames combined with the monotonous sound of sleet lightly tinkling on the windows to form a hypnotic effect that she couldn't resist. Her last coherent thought was that she hoped that the weather wouldn't cause Dan any problem in getting home and that maybe he would come home a little early. In just a few minutes, she was sound asleep on the couch.

She was awakened some time later by the ringing of her phone. It rang a couple of times before it fully registered with her brain. She groggily looked at the caller ID. It said "Nancy Fletcher". Good. She had been playing phone tag with Nancy. She quickly answered before it could go to voicemail. She said "Hey Nancy, give me a second here" as she sat up and put her feet on the floor. She sat there for a moment, rubbing her eyes and letting a few of the cobwebs clear. She looked at the clock on the mantel. It was 5:15 pm.

"Oh crap, It looks like I have been sleeping all afternoon and I haven't even started supper. Dan is going to kill me."

"Kill you? Now, that seems like a bit of an extreme reaction for such a mild mannered man. Or does he have a dark side that I am not aware of?"

Christine smiled. Nancy and her husband, John, had lived next door to Christine's apartment in Memphis. Nancy, who was several years older than Christine, had been a good friend of Christine's and had been something of a mentor as Christine had sought to draw closer in her walk with the Lord.

"Actually, that's what I wanted to talk to you about."

"You mean he does have a dark side?"

"No, no, hang on, I'm not articulating well. My brain is still a little fuzzy."

"Girl, you must have been really sleeping. Take a minute to get your head clear. Do I need to call back later?"

"No, I'm OK. I think I need some coffee."

"By all means, get some, and talk to me. What's on your mind? Is everything OK with you and Dan?"

As Christine made her way to the kitchen, she explained.

"Yes, things are good, but not as good as they could be."

"Why?"

"Roger."

"Roger? Is he giving you problems again?"

"No. I haven't heard from him or seen him."

"Then what's the problem?"

Christine told her of her hypersensitivity and feelings of inadequacy, where Dan was concerned, stemming from her history with Roger. She switched to her wireless Bluetooth headphones, so that she could work on supper while she talked. She told Nancy of her love for Dan and that, while she and Dan were close, she was troubled by the fact that there was this barrier that Roger had erected that kept them from getting closer.

"Roger put me through so much. I waited for so long, without even dating, because I thought that I couldn't move on because I didn't think that Roger and I really had biblical grounds for divorce. Then, I found out that he had cheated on me while we were married so we did have biblical grounds and I could move on but, still, really, I couldn't. I was so afraid that the next guy would turn out to be just like him. Then, I finally pushed past that fear and I found Dan. Dan is so wonderful and he loves me so much but I can't fully experience his love because Roger's darkness is still here."

As she spoke, Christine was getting out pots, pans, cooking utensils, and groceries. Her voice slowly took on an angry tone and she started slamming things around. A bit concerned, Nancy asked if she was OK. At that, Christine collapsed at the kitchen table and began to cry.

"I have everything I ever wanted and I can't just let go and accept it because of Roger. I hate him!"

There was silence, broken only by Christine's quiet sniffling. After a few seconds of silence, Nancy spoke.

"I would say that you don't really mean that but I'm sure that you do."

Very emphatically, Christine said "Yes I do".

"If I were in your place, I would probably feel the same way."

There was a long moment of silence.

"Because I do understand how you feel, I don't like to say this, but, Christine, as a Christian, you cannot hate, for any reason."

"I know that!"

It came out harsher than Christine intended.

"I'm sorry. I'm just a wreck at the moment."

"That's OK darlin'. I don't think that you have spoken harshly to me in the whole time I've known you. With what you're dealing with, you're entitled."

"I'm not entitled to snap at you for trying to help me with something that you had nothing to do with. The thing is, I know that I am not supposed to hate him and it makes me feel guilty that I do and that just makes me hate him even more."

"You have such a sweet spirit. Dan is a lucky man. It makes me hate the situation all the more."

There was a pause.

"I don't really know exactly what to tell you. I can quote scripture but that isn't what you need to hear right now. Have you talked to Brother Luke about this?"

"No, I haven't talked to anyone about it."

"Not even Dan?"

"No, especially not him."

"Well, you might want to talk to him. At least, then, he would know what is going on. It's probably worse for him to just wonder and imagine what the problem might be. Anyway, I bet he would be very understanding. He seems to be that kind of guy."

"You're probably right. I will talk to him, but not tonight."

"No, not tonight. Also, you should talk to Brother Luke. I'm sure that you won't be the first person to come to him with a similar story and he can advise you spiritually much better than I."

"I don't know about that. You do pretty well yourself. I will talk to him too. Thank you. It feels much better just getting it out."

"You're welcome. Any time. Can I pray with you?"

"Of course."

After talking to Nancy, Christine did feel much better. She no longer felt like cooking though. After talking to Dan and finding out that he would be home in about an hour, she ordered pizza. She was a little surprised to find that they were still delivering, with the worsening road conditions, but she was glad they were. While she waited for the pizza to be delivered, she sat back down in front of the fire. After a moment, she began to pray.

"Lord, I thank you for bringing Dan into my life. Please give him safe travel home tonight. Right now, I don't really know what to ask you for concerning my Roger issues. Please just help me to deal with the situation and please help it not to damage my relationship with Dan or with you. I love you Father. Please help me. Amen."

Chapter 11

As Dan turned onto his street, his truck slid just a little, startling him out of his thoughts about the events of the day. What a day it had been. As his house came into view, his thoughts shifted to Christine and he had a longing to see her, to share with her about his day and to hear her thoughts about it. He knew that she would have a meaningful prospective, cutting through the crap and getting to the heart of the matter, helping to clarify things. She always did. That was one of the many things that he loved about her. An unconscious smile spread across his face.

As he turned into his driveway, the truck slid again and he wondered if he should have borrowed Jake's truck, which was equipped with four wheel drive. He thought about that for a moment as he sat in his garage, looking in his mirror at the snow and sleet that was still falling on the driveway. Should he go swap trucks with Jake? Jake didn't have his license yet and so couldn't drive the truck anyway. He quickly dismissed the thought. When he had dropped Jake off a few minutes ago, Jake's mood had improved slightly from what it had been earlier but he was still very withdrawn. Dan decided that it was better to just leave him alone for a while and let him sort through things. He would talk to Dan when he was ready. In the meantime, it was probably better to just stay away and give him space. If they were snowed in the next day, which appeared very likely, so much the better. That would give him and Jake a little time apart and it would give Dan some much needed time to think.

With that decided, his longing to see Christine returned. He also suddenly noticed how hungry he was. He hadn't eaten anything since his lunch meeting with Mike.

He found Christine in the kitchen.

"Hey, I'm starving. What kind of pizza did you get?"

Christine quickly kissed him and laughed.

"That's the first thing that you say to me? Well, I love you too."

Dan laughed too.

"I love you if you got my favorite pizza."

"Well, why don't you look and see."

He adopted a playful tone.

"Where is it, where is it, where is it!"

She smiled.

"I thought we could relax and eat in the living room. It's on the coffee table. Your drink is there too, hungry guy. It was just delivered about ten minutes ago so it's still hot."

"Yay!"

Using large exaggerated motions, he playfully ran into the living room. This kind of banter and silliness was often a part of his and Christine's interaction and Dan loved it. He loved her keen intellect and insight into the important matters of life but he also loved being able to relax and have fun with her. On the coffee table, he found two pizza boxes (his favorite and her favorite), two soft drinks and two plates. Soft music was playing and the gas logs in the fireplace were turned up. He could hear the sleet tinkling against the windows even harder now. Oh yes, they were definitely going to get snowed in and that sounded pretty good right now. The stress of the day lifted. With a playful flourish, he grabbed a piece of pizza and stuffed half of it into his mouth. With a mouth full, he said "Who needs home cooking when you've got pizza".

He turned, expecting to see Christine laughing or, at least, smiling. Instead, her expression was hard to read but appeared to be somewhat somber. Dan was puzzled.

"Are you OK?"

"Yeah, sure."

"You don't look OK and your mood has changed. You look so serious all of a sudden. What's wrong?"

"Nothing. I guess I'm just hungry."

But Dan knew that she wasn't just hungry. He suddenly got it. "When I said what I said about home cooking, did you think that I was criticizing you for not cooking tonight?"

"I would have cooked but I fell asleep on the couch and then Nancy called and"

"Hey hey hey, it's OK. It's fine that you didn't cook. You know I love pizza. Would I have been prancing around in here like an idiot if I was upset?"

"No, I guess not."

She smiled weakly but her mood wasn't nearly as buoyant as it had been before. Dan felt the stress that had previously lifted descend once again. He said "I'm going to change before I eat" and he quickly disappeared back into their bed room. He was glad that Christine didn't follow him and, with the sudden downward shift in her mood, he hadn't expected her to. He needed a minute alone. What was it with her? He loved her more than anything in the world but these sudden down turns in her mood were very frustrating. He didn't really understand it. It appeared to happen when she perceived that he had slighted her or criticized her in some way. The thing was, he never openly criticized her. Really, the only thing in her that he found fault with was this near obsession with church. That and these funny mood shifts. But he had only mentioned the church thing to Mike and he had mentioned the mood shifts to no one. He certainly hadn't mentioned any of it to Christine. Why was she so quick to think that he was upset with her. He supposed that her history with Roger might have something to do with it. Perhaps he should try to talk to her about the situation. He shook his head. Yet another thing to worry about.

When he went back into the living room, he found Christine sitting on the couch. She patted the seat beside her. As he sat down, she spoke.

"I want to talk to you about something and I don't want you to interrupt."

He nodded.

"It's about the way that I acted a few minutes ago. The way my mood changed.

He nodded again.

"You know that I went through a lot of things with Roger. He ended up being horrible to me. In the beginning, though, he wasn't horrible. If he had been, I wouldn't have married him. At first, he was great. Then he slowly changed. I don't know if he just hid his true nature at first or if his mental instability worsened over time. Either way, we were married for a little while before I started to glimpse a darkness in him."

Suddenly, Dan understood and his heart ached for Christine and what she was going through.

"And you are afraid that I will turn out to have a dark side too."

She smiled weakly.

"I thought you weren't going to interrupt."

"Sorry. Couldn't help myself."

They sat in silence for a few seconds before she continued.

"In my heart, I know that you could never be like Roger but sometimes my head lags a little behind my heart."

She reached out and took his hand as she started to cry.

"Please don't be hurt. I don't mean to be this way and I'm trying to work on it. I love you so much. I don't want this to come between us."

Dan reached out and took her in his arms.

"I love you more than anything. We will work through it together. I'm glad that you told me."

She pulled back, her tears diminishing.

"I should have told you before now. I just wasn't sure how you would react and I had no idea what to do about it. That's what I was talking to Nancy about today."

"Did she have any words of wisdom?"

"She said that I should talk to you."

"Smart girl."

"She also said that I should talk to Brother Luke."

"Can't hurt".

"Oh boy", Dan thought, "Here we go with the church thing again" but she said little else about it.

After just a little bit more discussion, they both seemed to want to decompress and move on to less weighty subjects for the rest of the night. Dan decided to wait to bring up the Vision Biotech issues later. They started eating and reminiscing about the weather and the fun that both of them had in the occasional winter storm as children growing up in West Tennessee. Eventually, they found a movie on TV and fell asleep cuddled up under a blanket on the couch.

On Friday morning, they found that 11 inches of snow had fallen and two inches of sleet. Perhaps not that big a deal in the northern climates but, here in West Tennessee, it qualified as a blizzard. With the high forecast to be in the low twenties, the snow wasn't going anywhere and neither were they. Christine prepared a big breakfast of eggs, bacon, and pancakes. After they ate, they settled in the living room, each of them with a big steaming cup of coffee.

"As much as I believe in Vision Biotech and what it's doing, I sure am glad to have a day off. All the pressures that go with getting it going are getting pretty rough."

"I can imagine. You haven't talked about the company much in the last few days. How are things going with it? Don't worry, I won't want to talk about it all day. I know this is a much needed day off for you."

"That's OK. I have some company related things that I want to talk to you about anyway."

He told her of the financial struggles, Jake's issues with reverse engineering, and Ben's desire to come to work for Vision Biotech. Christine did not interrupt and, when he had finished, Dan could almost see the gears turning in her head. After a couple minutes, she spoke.

"Well, about the financial problems. Do you think that you could get a loan if you can't get all three of the gold patients?"

"Probably so. Mike and I are working on that. We won't be able to borrow all of it though so we will need at least one gold patient, preferably two. I think that we can get two, especially if we cut the price, which we could do if we are going to borrow part of the money. So, yeah, I think that we can handle the financial angle."

"And that is based on numbers that don't take into account any money that you would save through Ben's involvement?"

"That is correct. Ben would save us some money and probably some time, especially if he can eliminate the need for reverse engineering, but, at least from a financial perspective, we could do it without him. After all, to this point, we hadn't planned on having him."

They sat in silence for a moment and then Christine spoke.

"I don't trust Ben. You don't either. He would save some money but, financially, it could be done without him. So, really, the decision about Ben all comes down to Jake and the reverse engineering issue."

"Yes, I suppose it does. Without Ben's help, I don't see any way around having to reverse engineer one of Jake's implants in order to get certain information about the design that we just can't get any other way."

"And, really, we don't even know for sure that Ben has the necessary information to keep from having to do the reverse engineering."

"That's true, we don't know for sure."

"Well, I certainly can understand Jake feeling the way that he does but it sounds like the best solution would be for him to agree to the reverse engineering."

"That's for sure."

"Clearly, before this goes any further, you need to talk to Jake."

Dan sighed heavily.

"Yeah, you're right. That's a conversation that I dread."

Chapter 12

Dan sat at the desk in his study and inhaled the aroma of the steam rising from the cup of coffee sitting in front of him. It had been a very nice and relatively stress free day. After the conversation about the problems that he was facing with Vision Biotech, he and Christine had spent the morning sitting in the living room, talking about everything in the world, none of it of much consequence, at least not to their day to day lives. They had been doing what his dad would call "solving the world's problems". Dan had really enjoyed the chance to just relax and not have to problem solve.

Now, after lunch, Christine was taking a nap and Dan was sitting here, deep in thought. When Dan looked out the window across from his desk that looked out onto the back yard, he saw that it had begun to snow again. It was a light snow, with big flakes but few of them, slowly drifting lazily down onto the existing thick blanket of white. It looked very serene. Dan found himself thinking that he might not mind joining Christine in her nap. He didn't think that sleep would come though, with all the thoughts swirling through his brain. In all of their conversation this morning, nothing had come up regarding Christianity and Dan was thankful for that. None the less, Dan was sitting here thinking about it. One thing had always struck Dan about Christine, including this morning. He wasn't exactly sure what to call it. She was so generous and humble, with a quiet strength. She was so loving. Not just romantic love. There was a deeper love that seemed to be instilled in her. She had a joy and a peace about her that seemed to be independent of her circumstances and surroundings. All in all, whatever it might be called, there was a quality about her that he had rarely seen in others. He couldn't help but wonder if this came from her faith.

He thought about some of the things that, in his mind, set her apart from most other people that he had known. She gave so freely of herself, not just at the church, though she did do a lot to help out there.

When old Mr. Tyler, down the street, had surgery and couldn't get out of bed for two weeks, Christine had taken him three meals a day for the entire two weeks. She had also cleaned his house and gotten Dan to cut his yard. She said that he had no family and no church to take care of him and someone needed to help him. Dan knew that the impetus for that had something to do with church because he remembered that she had said something about ministering and being salt and light. He hadn't paid that much attention because, at the time, it sounded to him like a bunch of religious mumbo-jumbo that didn't really mean anything. Now, though, he was starting to wonder.

Christine had also started working on the preliminaries to put together a foundation that would raise money to pay for those who had no insurance to benefit from Vision Biotech's technology. Putting together something like that was very noble and it required a lot of networking and trying to garner publicity. There was plenty of opportunity for Christine to seek praise for her efforts and in deed much was offered but she always seemed uncomfortable with it. Where possible, she preferred to work quietly, behind the scenes. Privately, she had said something about "I must decrease that He may increase". More religious mumbo-jumbo? Something deeper with real meaning? Dan didn't know.

Dan had no illusions that one had to have religion to be generous or to help others. Dan had helped others out plenty. Look at what he had done for Jake. He had literally spent millions for Jake's benefit. He hadn't helped anyone else out quite that much but he had helped out many friends and employees, over the years, and he was happy to do it. It made

46

Dan feel good to help others. Still, with Christine, it was different. He couldn't quite put his finger on it.

She also didn't seem to get as outwardly rattled by life's little stresses as many people did. She never swore, never yelled, and rarely even showed apparent exasperation.

Not that she was perfect. It was true that the issues that had been caused by the way that Roger had treated her did seem to upset her serenity and was even affecting their relationship. Dan certainly didn't hold that against her, though. His heart ached for her and all that she had endured because of Roger. In fact, despite his fledgling private interest in Christianity, that was one problem that Dan had with the whole Christianity thing. Why God would let someone like Christine get mixed up with someone like Roger and go through what she had as a result. If God was real and if he really cared about His children, then things like that just didn't make any sense.

Dan sat back and continued to watch the snow fall. He was struck by the beauty just outside his window. Surely God did exist. A world like this could not have come into existence simply by chance, through a bunch of random events. As an analytical person and a numbers guy, Dan knew that, statistically and objectively, that was impossible.

Then Dan thought about Mike Hannon. Many of the rare qualities that Dan so admired in Christine were also present in Mike and Mike too was a Christian. Coincidence? Dan thought perhaps not.

Dan stood and took a dusty bible off of one of the shelves behind his desk. He sat back down and placed the bible on the desk in front of him. Where to start? He had no idea what he was even looking for. He thought "Well, I guess, start at the beginning". He opened the Bible and read.

"In the beginning God created the heavens and the earth."

Dan shook his head. No, way too basic. He thought "If God exists, and surely He does, I know that He created the Earth."

Dan thought he would skip to the end and see what was there. He read.

"The grace of our Lord Jesus Christ be with you all. Amen." Hmmm. Still not exactly what Dan was looking for but this seemed closer. He backed up one verse.

"He who testifies to these things says, "Surely I am coming quickly." Amen. Even so, come, Lord Jesus!"

Yes, Dan had heard Christine talk about Jesus coming back. Heck, for that matter, he had heard people talk about "the second coming" in slang, as in "This is taking forever, we will be here until the second coming". Interesting, sort of, but it didn't help him any.

Dan closed the Bible. He was just getting more confused. Where could he get answers? He thought about looking around on the internet but he thought that would be confusing as well, with all of the various religious view points out there. He decided that he would take a practical approach. When he had a drippy faucet, he called a plumber. When he was sick, he consulted a doctor. Now, he had questions about religion so he would call a preacher, Christine's preacher, Brother Luke, the man who had married him and Christine. He quickly found the number and dialed, before he changed his mind.

Chapter 13

Saturday morning, James Swanson sat and stared at the letter that he had just received. It was just what he had hoped for and it had come sooner than he had ever thought. This could be the answer to his problems.

James had been the head lab tech at Biotronics when the company had manufactured the artificial retinal implants which had given Jake Richardson his eyesight. James had helped to oversee the project and so he had a great deal of knowledge concerning the inner workings of the implants. That knowledge had been used to sabotage the implants at the behest of Steve Levitt, a "fixer" who worked for the health insurance industry. The industry hadn't been happy about all of the money that they were about to have to pay out on behalf of thousands of blind people, in the event of a successful clinical trial of the implants. So, the industry had set out, through Steve, to make sure that the first clinical trial was not a success. Steve had caught James at a particularly low point, financially, and had offered him money to sabotage the left implant by reprograming it. The plan was thwarted when Jake had accidentally discovered the reprogramming before the implant was activated. So, James was caught before he had received any of the money, other than a very small advance. Now, as a result, here he sat in jail with a ten year sentence, more broke than ever, and with a wife who was threatening to leave him.

Today, his wife, Beth, had planned to visit, as she did every Saturday, but she had been unable to do so. Because of the winter weather, some of the guards had not been able to make it to work and the prison officials had felt that having visitation with a less than full guard staff would present an unjustifiable level of danger. Besides, the same winter weather that had kept some of the guards home would probably keep almost all of the visitors home as well. A few of the people in his cell block had grumbled about the cancelation of visitation (they would grumble about anything) but it was just fine with James. Beth had grown increasingly cold toward him and, every Saturday, he feared that she would tell him that she was leaving him. He didn't mind delaying that possibility for another week.

As he thought about his plight, James frowned, but then he looked at the letter in his hand and he couldn't help but smile. He had put in place an insurance policy of sorts and it was about to pay off. He had "accidentally" withheld a little bit of information from the records of Biotronics and he had that information privately stashed away. Not much really. Just a few details concerning the design of one component. With enough time and money, the component could be reverse engineered from the prototype implants. Of course, that would also require a willing implant recipient. At the time, he hadn't even known why he had done it. He just thought that it might come in handy one day, especially if things didn't go as planned with Steve. Well, things hadn't gone as planned and here he was.

He looked down at the letter, at one paragraph in particular. "There is key information missing from the project records concerning the design of the tertiary optical transducer. I noticed this omission early in the project and had intended to pursue it but never got around to it. Without this information, additional implants cannot be manufactured. I believe that you have this information. I know you to be too careful a scientist to have simply not recorded it. Of course, the prototype implants can be reverse engineered but that will take a lot of time and a lot more money. In order to avoid that, I am willing to compensate you fairly if you have the needed information and have the means to get it to me."

James contemplated. A dollar figure was not specified. James didn't like that. He is willing to pay me fairly. Hmmm,

50

"fairly", a very subjective term. James knew that getting the information through reverse engineering would probably cost at least a million and that was assuming that the implant recipient was willing to allow the implants to be reverse engineered. James figured that getting the information from him should be worth at least a quarter of a million, maybe even half a million.

Still holding the letter, James laid back on the bunk in his cell and thought about the situation. One thing puzzled him. His eyes moved down to the signature. "Ben Nelson". Why was Ben seeking this information? Unless James was not mistaken, and he knew that he wasn't, Ben no longer owned Vision Biotech. Everything surrounding the melt down of Vision Biotech, including Ben's selling out, had been well covered in the media. James could understand the Richardsons being willing to pay for the information but why in the world did Ben want it? He couldn't be going to work for a competitor of Vision Biotech. Ben had sold the patents on the technology along with the company. That too had been covered in the media. In the end, James supposed that it really didn't matter why Ben wanted the information, so long as he was willing and able to pay for it. Still, James didn't understand what was going on and he didn't like being in situations that he didn't fully understand. He said aloud "Doctor Ben Nelson, what are you up to".

After an hour of thoughtful contemplation he got up and began to draft his response to Ben and also a letter to Beth.

Chapter 14

Monday morning, Jake's room was filled with the sound of a bell tower. He picked up his iPhone and silenced it. Three months after gaining his eyesight, he was still amazed at his ability to look at the screen of the phone in order to use it, rather than relying on screen reading technology. By using Voice Over, Apple's built in screen reader, even as a blind man, Jake had been able to do just about anything with an iPhone that sighted people could do. But actually looking at the screen was just so cool.

Being able to look at his phone was the least of the ways that his life had changed in the last three months. He thought about that as he made his way down the hall to the kitchen to start the coffee. As the coffee brewed, he looked out the window of his kitchen door, out into the garage, at the brand new black Chevrolet Silverado, loaded, with grey leather interior. As he gazed at it, he could practically smell the leather. He decided that he wanted to smell it for real. He placed his hand on the biometric reader just to the right of the door. He thought that Dan might have been overly cautious in insisting that Jake's home have the same security as did Dan's and Christine's but it wasn't really that much trouble and Dan had paid for it. As Jake made his way to the driver's door of the truck and opened it, he thought about Dan. He felt bad about the way that things had gone the other day. Dan had done so much for him and, really, Dan was just doing the best that he could with the circumstances that he had been given. Jake grasped the handle on the ceiling of the truck, just inside the door, planted his foot on the running board, and swung himself up into the driver's seat. His eyes swept across the gage cluster, to the stereo and AC controls and then up to the windshield. He and Dan had planned to start driving lessons this week. Shortly, he would be driving this thing, with Dan in the passenger seat. Then, a little later, he would be driving alone.

He thought about the independence that this truck would afford him, independence unlike he had ever known. He thought about driving himself to and from work. He thought about going to lunch, on his own, when he was hungry. He thought about going to places like Wal-Mart and even eventually taking road trips. How awesome was that going to be? And could he take a chance on losing it?

If he let them take out his implants to reverse engineer them, how long would he be without sight? He shivered at the thought. And what if something went wrong? What if the implants were to be damaged? What if the re-implantation procedure went wrong? What if he never saw again? What if he had received this wonderful gift just to lose it again? At the thought, his pulse began to quicken and he began to perspire. What was this? Was he starting to have a panic attack? Seriously? What was wrong with him? He quickly exited the truck and went back in the house.

He went into the bathroom and splashed cold water on his face. He quickly calmed down but his reaction bothered him. He poured himself a large mug of black coffee and sat down at the desk in his study to think.

He had been blind for years and he had faced a lot of hardship as a result. Still, he had made it fine. So why was he panicky at the thought of very unlikely complications in a procedure that he hadn't even committed to undergo? If he did this, everything would almost certainly go fine and tens of thousands would benefit. Jake was an avid Star Trek fan and he thought of the words of Spock. "The needs of the many outweigh the needs of the few or the one." Didn't the Bible say something like that too? He might have to ask Dan, though he didn't think that Dan knew much more about the Bible than Jake did. Anyway, the whole "good of the many" thing sounded good in theory and Jake even knew that he really should feel that way but he just didn't and couldn't. The way that he felt bothered him but that was just the way that it was. Surely there was another way and Dan would just have to find it.

Jake decided that he would talk to Dan when he came to pick Jake up for work. Then he remembered that there would be no work today. Though there had been no more snow since late Saturday, the temperatures still hovered below freezing and today was to be cloudy so even the sun wouldn't help to melt the existing cover of snow and ice. Jake doubted that he and Dan would be going to work until at least Wednesday. Well, both of them had well equipped studies at home and they could get a lot done without ever leaving the house. Even working at home would require them to communicate though, and Jake didn't want this hanging over them. He decided to go ahead and call Dan and tell him of his decision. As Jake dialed, his gut tightened. He knew that Dan would and should expect better from him. He didn't like disappointing Dan but it would be OK. They would find another way. They had to.

Chapter 15

Thursday afternoon, Christine sat in her car in the parking lot of Emmanuel Baptist Church. She had an appointment with Pastor Luke Stanley, who had performed her and Dan's wedding ceremony, three months previous. This morning, she had called to set up an appointment to talk to Brother Luke about the issues that she was having with the way that Roger had treated her and how that was effecting her relationship with Dan. That appointment was at 1 pm, five minutes from now.

Christine was nervous but she wasn't really sure why. Of course, she didn't enjoy talking about her past with Roger but Brother Luke had been very friendly in church and she was sure that he would be very understanding now. Still, she dreaded this meeting. She spent another moment in silent prayer and then she got out of her car and went in.

Christine found the church secretary, Bettie Lawson, at her desk. As she approached, Christine could hear voices coming from Brother Luke's open door, just behind Betty.

"Oh, does he have someone in there? Maybe I got the time mixed up."

"Oh, no, it's fine. Katie is in there. Brother Luke said to tell you to go on in when you got here."

"Oh, OK, thanks."

Christine was puzzled. Katie was Brother Luke's wife, a very nice person, but why was she in the office if Brother Luke knew that he had an appointment with Christine? As Christine entered the office, Both Brother Luke and Katie stood. Brother Luke shook Christine's hand and Katie gave her a quick hug. When Brother Luke and Christine sat, so did Katie. Apparently she was staying. Christine's puzzlement and nervousness grew.

"First, let me explain why Katie is here. Early in my ministry, I made a policy never to be alone with a woman, other than my wife, anywhere, for any reason. It isn't that I don't trust you and it isn't that I don't trust me."

Katie broke in.

"And it isn't that I don't trust either of you."

There was light laughter.

"It is best to avoid even the slightest temptation and even the possible appearance of any impropriety."

Christine nodded.

"I understand."

And indeed she did but she still didn't like it.

Katie lightly touched Christine's hand and spoke.

"Let me assure you. Sitting in on Luke's counseling sessions with women is something that I do regularly and I hold everything that I hear in strict confidence. This is one way that I help to support Luke's ministry. Regardless of what you say, I will not repeat it and I will not judge you for it. Just pretend that I am not here."

Easier said than done. Christine did feel better about Katie's presence now though. She nodded again and offered Katie a weak smile.

Now, it was again Brother Luke's turn to speak.

"So, Christine, tell me what's on your mind."

It took a while to get going but, after a few minutes, Christine found herself getting more comfortable and she found herself pouring out her soul. She told Brother Luke everything, of Rogers courtship, their marriage, the good months early on, the trouble that eventually ensued, the divorce, finding Dan, and the shadow that her past with Roger was now casting over her and Dan's relationship. She said "I hate Roger for the effect that he still has on me and for the effect that it is having on my and Dan's relationship".

When she had finished, Brother Luke sat in contemplative silence for a moment before speaking.

"First of all, I want to assure you that what you are feeling is quite normal, both in terms of how Roger's past treatment still makes you feel and in terms of your feelings toward Roger because of that. You aren't ridiculously paranoid because you are afraid that Dan could end up being like Roger. You aren't some horrible person because you hate Roger for doing this to you. You are normal and you are doing the best you can with the situation. Don't beat yourself up over this. OK?"

With tears on her face, Christine nodded weakly.

"Now, with that said, as Christians, we are not justified to hate for any reason. I'm sure you know that and I do not say that to judge but rather to establish a bit of a foundation for what I am about to tell you."

Christine remained silent and nodded very slightly.

"The bible says, in Mark 12:31, "You shall love your neighbor as yourself". This can be the hardest commandment to keep but doing so is absolutely vital to your fellowship with God. The Bible says, in 1 John 4:20, that we cannot hate one another and yet love God. Hate can destroy your fellowship with God. It not only can but it will. I can tell you this from personal experience."

"Really? You? Hatred?"

"Yes. Me. Hatred. Are you surprised? Because I am a pastor?"

"Well, um, yes, a little, I guess." Christine looked embarrassed.

"I am a pastor but I am also human. I am a sinner, saved by grace, just like you."

Christine was intrigued. She knew that, like her, pastors were also sinners, saved by grace, but she had never really thought about their human side before. Perhaps that was because many of them kept their guard up, not letting their human side show.

Brother Luke continued.

"You know Blake."

"Yes, of course."

Blake was the oldest of the Stanley's three children. He was confined to a wheel chair, a total paraplegic, but he didn't let that slow him down. From what Christine could tell, he was very involved in all of the church youth activities and he seemed to live life to the fullest. He seemed to see his disability as an inconvenience to be dealt with, albeit a big one, and deal with it he did. In that way, he reminded Christine of Jake, living life to the fullest despite his blindness, before he had gained his eyesight through the technology of Vision Biotech.

"Do you know how he came to be in that wheel chair?"

Christine shook her head.

"We were on our way home from church one night. Blake was sitting in the back on the passenger side. As I pulled out of the parking lot, a drunk driver ran the light and hit us at 60 miles per hour."

Christine gasped.

"It was only he and I in the car that night. Katie was home sick and the younger kids had stayed at church to participate in a children's bible study. I was going to come back and get them later. I was shaken but OK. Blake almost didn't survive. He was air lifted to Vanderbilt Hospital in Nashville."

"I had no idea. That's horrible."

"I pray that you never find out firsthand how horrible that really is. He had multiple surgeries to repair several internal injuries. Finally, after about a week, it was apparent that he would survive but that he would never walk again."

As Luke described Blake's injuries, she saw Katie tear up. Obviously, reliving these events was very painful, even now. Christine's heart went out to them and she unconsciously put her hand to her mouth as she tried to imagine their anguish. Though she and Dan didn't yet have children, they wanted them, and she could not imagine one day watching a child of hers go through what they were describing.

60

"The car that hit us was driven by Dennis Feldman."

"I have never heard of him but I have only lived in Jackson for a few months."

"He doesn't live around here anymore anyway. He served a five year sentence for DUI and vehicular assault. After he got out, he moved to Montgomery, Alabama."

"I guess that's good. I mean I guess you are glad you don't have to see him around."

"From the time of the accident, I hated him for what he had done and, from a worldly prospective, I was absolutely justified. For about two years, until I let go of the hatred, this destroyed my fellowship with God. My prayers didn't seem to get higher than the ceiling, I had no joy, and my ministry did not grow. I didn't fully realize what the problem was until God had taken the hatred from me. And He did take the hatred from me because I, myself, could not let go of it. I tried. Well, I sort of tried. Deep down, I didn't want to let go of it. I knew that this hatred was a sin and that it caused Jesus to bear a great deal more suffering on my behalf. Still, I could not or would not let go of it. I came to a point where I had to ask God to forgive me for everything that I had put Him through as a result of this hatred and, broken before Him, I finally sincerely asked him to take it from me. He did."

All Christine could say was "wow".

"You are harboring hatred in your heart toward Roger and you must get rid of it. If you can't, and you probably can't, you must ask God to take it. If you sincerely ask, He will take it. From a human perspective, you are completely justified in feeling the way that you feel. I was too. But I'm telling you that you cannot feel that way and enjoy fellowship with God. Until you leave the hatred behind, you will never truly fulfill God's purpose for your life."

There was silence for several seconds before Christine spoke. "It will be hard but not as hard as what you have described."

"Well, don't underestimate the significance of your own pain. Emotional scars are just as real and just as valid as physical ones. I'm sorry that I have no easy answers for you. The bottom line is that the only way for you to move on past this and make the most of your and Dan's marriage is with God and the only way to enjoy his fellowship is through love, not hate. Start by spending a lot of time in prayer. Many people have certain activities that make them feel closer to God. Is there anything like that for you?

"Well, I really enjoy sewing. I have made a lot of my own clothes and I spend a lot of time thinking and praying when I am working at my sewing machine."

"OK, that's good. Plan to spend some time alone, just you, your sewing machine, and God. I like getting alone with God in nature, sometimes in a deer stand. When I was trying to work through my pain relating to the situation with Blake, I filled two chest freezers with venison. Maybe you can fill a closet or two."

Though Brother Luke hadn't offered any easy and quick solutions, Christine was feeling more hopeful.

"Well, from the Cross, Jesus forgave those who crucified him. If He can do that, surely I can forgive Roger. I don't see how right now but I will try to get alone with God as much as I can and ask Him to help me."

"Yes, do that. Also spend time in bible study. Getting in the Word regularly is important for any Christian at any time and it is especially crucial when facing something like this. Ask God to reveal new and relevant spiritual truths to you. He often uses tribulation to draw us closer to Him. I know that it's really hard right now but I think that you will find that, in the end, your faith will be strengthened through this."

They talked a little more and, as Christine left, she felt much better. As she got in her car, she was reminded of Philippians 4:13, "I can do all things through Christ who strengthens me".

Chapter 16

Dan pulled out of the parking lot of Vision Biotech and headed for Emmanuel Baptist Church. He still couldn't believe that he was going to talk to a pastor about Christianity. It wasn't that he was ashamed of it. He wasn't. He just had never been what he thought of as "the religious type" and he never thought that he would ever have much interest in religion but, for some reason, he had found himself thinking about it more and more lately. He supposed that the reason was the difference that he had noticed in both Christine and Mike Hannon, two of the people whom he respected most in the world and two people who he knew to be Christians. It seemed that there might have been something else drawing his interest too, something that he couldn't quite put his finger on.

His thoughts were interrupted as he pulled into the church parking lot. Was that Christine pulling out? Nah, surely not. He hadn't told Christine that he was meeting with Luke. He wasn't hiding it but he didn't want her bugging him about it later. It probably hadn't been her and, even if it was, she was probably just here about something that she was doing for the church. She was always doing something for the church. He wasn't as inclined to judge that as harshly as he once had. After all, wasn't he here because of the qualities that he had seen in her? Because of the way that she lived her life? Obviously, whatever she was doing was working. Maybe he was about to find out more about that.

Betty greeted Dan warmly and ushered him into Brother Luke's office. Dan's initial impression was positive. Luke was of medium height and build, clean shaven, with sandy blond hair. He sat behind a relatively small, cluttered desk, with an open bible on the corner. When he stood to greet Dan, his smile was warm and his hand shake firm.

"Hello Mr. Richardson. Welcome to Emmanuel Baptist Church. I am Luke Stanley, the pastor. It's a pleasure to meet you. I have heard a lot of good things about you from Christine."

"And some bad things I bet."

"Yes, but I only believe the good things."

Both men laughed. As Dan sat, he surveyed the room. It wasn't what he would have expected. The room was not all that large, perhaps 12 by 12, and there was nothing ornate about it. On two walls, there were large book cases, practically overflowing. Behind the desk, there was a credenza with a phone and a laptop computer. Above the credenza, there was a wooden cross and below it was a framed verse, John 14:6, which read "I am the way, the truth, and the life: no one comes to the Father, except by me". Other than that and the bible on the desk, this could have been taken for just any ordinary office anywhere. It looked much like most of the offices at R and R Accounting, the accounting firm that he had founded in Atlanta. Dan had expected something more ornate, something fancier, something that conveyed holiness and made the man behind the desk seem something less than completely approachable. Dan found it comforting that this was not the case. Maybe this wouldn't be so bad.

Brother Luke clapped his hands together and then held them clasped in front of him for a brief moment as a smile spread across his face. Here was more of the joy that Dan had seen in Christine and Mike. Brother Luke leaned back slightly, taking on a relaxed posture as he began to speak.

"So, you have questions about Christianity. Where shall I start? As you called me, I would assume that you have specific questions that you would like me to address."

Dan wasn't quite sure where to begin.

"Well, yes. First of all, you must understand that this is all relatively new to me."

Brother Luke nodded.

"I gathered that from what you said on the phone and that's fine."

"My parents are good people, great people actually. They raised me well but they did not raise me in church. In fact, we never went."

Dan paused. Luke nodded again but did not interrupt.

"I feel like I am a pretty good person. I don't drink or do drugs. I have never cheated on my spouse or even wanted to. I work hard. I have done pretty well, financially, and I have used my money to help others, when I have found opportunity. Don't get me wrong, I know that I am not perfect, but I think I'm a pretty good guy."

Again, Dan paused. Again, Luke nodded but did not interrupt.

"Recently, I have begun to feel like something is missing. Well, not missing exactly, but I have seen things in Christine that I don't have and she is a Christian. At first, she drove me nuts with all of her churchiness. Um, no offense."

Luke grinned.

"So, anyway, I have noticed a lot of little things about her that are different from most people that I have known. I have noticed those same qualities in Mike Hannon, an old friend and colleague, and he is also a Christian. I'm starting to wonder, for both he and Christine, if their faith is what makes the difference in them."

Dan went on to explain, the best he could. Luke nodded occasionally but seemed content to let Dan talk, without interruption. When it was clear that Dan had said all that he wanted to say for the moment, Luke spoke.

"I know Christine to be a strong Christian, doing her best to live out her faith. It sounds like the same is true of your friend, Mike."

Dan nodded.

"So, how can I help you? Shall I take you through the plan of salvation? In other words, do you want to know how to become a Christian, like Christine and Mike?"

Dan shook his head.

"No, not yet. Maybe later. First, before I know exactly what they believe, I want to know more about why they believe it."

"Sure, I can help you with that."

"Good. First of all, I assume that everything that you, and they, believe is rooted in the Bible?"

"Yes."

"So, how do you know what the Bible says is true? Take Jesus for example. I assume that it was Jesus who said what is there in that frame above your head."

Luke nodded.

"As I have said, I am certainly no Bible scholar, but I assume that Jesus was saying there that He is the only way to God and the only way to Heaven."

"Yes, that is exactly what He was saying."

"But how do you know that He even existed? I mean, the Bible says that He existed but, other than that, if you don't just take the Bible at face value, how do you know? Please understand, I mean no disrespect to you or your beliefs. I'm just trying to understand."

Luke smiled very broadly.

"I perceive no disrespect at all on your part. Your question is a very common one and it is something that even some of my members probably struggle with from time to time."

Luke sat forward, warming to his subject.

"We know that Jesus existed because His existence is more thoroughly documented than any other figure in history, even if you completely discount the Bible."

Dan's interest was piqued. He had never heard this before. Luke continued.

"Jesus was written of by the Jewish historian, Josephus, and by the Roman historian, Tacitus. In addition, there are writings by many non-historians which mention Jesus. Some of these people were very anti-Christian. In fact, some of them actively persecuted Christians and even killed them because of their faith. And yet, even these people who killed those who followed Jesus did not deny the existence of Jesus."

Dan was fascinated.

"Today, even among non-Christians, there is near unanimity among scholars that Jesus really lived and that he was crucified by order of the Roman Prefect Pontius Pilate."

Dan was stunned. There really was proof of some of this stuff. Luke continued.

"Now then, the central tenants of our faith are based on not just the crucifixion but on the resurrection, that is that, after being crucified, Jesus rose from the dead on the third day."

Dan nodded.

"I've heard about the resurrection, though I don't entirely understand the significance of it."

"We will deal with the significance of it in a few minutes. For now, let's just focus on the fact of it."

Dan nodded again.

"It is not possible to definitively prove that the resurrection occurred. Many believe that the Shroud of Turin offers proof. Are you familiar with the Shroud?"

"I have heard of it but I know little about it."

"It is a piece of ancient linen which bears the image of a man who appears to have suffered physical trauma that is consistent with what we know of the crucifixion of Jesus. Many believe that this is the burial shroud of Jesus, that there are supernatural elements related to the creation of the image, and that this proves that the resurrection occurred. However, there is debate as to how the image was formed and there has been radio carbon dating which dates the Shroud to a time that is much more recent than the time of Jesus. Because of these things, the authenticity of the Shroud as the burial shroud of Jesus is not universally accepted. Ultimately, there is no definitive proof that the resurrection occurred."

"Hmmm, I see."

"Now hold on. There is not scientific proof. However, the gospel, that is the story of Jesus' life including the resurrection, had spread around the world within 60 years after the crucifixion. Bear in mind, this occurred without all of the information technology and means of travel that we have now. Would the impetus of such a movement have been based on events that did not really occur?"

Dan shook his head.

"Not at all likely."

"That isn't all. I suspect that you have heard of the disciples of Jesus."

"Yes, I think there were 12 of them."

"That is correct. These 12 men were with Jesus continually during his earthly ministry, which is the last three years of His life. They saw Jesus crucified, they watched Him die, and they saw Him after he arose from the dead. One of these 12 men, Judas, hung himself after having played a part in the arrest and crucifixion. After the suicide of Judas, he was replaced by another man who had been with Jesus, so there were again 12 disciples."

"Interesting."

"Yes, but there is something even more interesting. Of these 12 men, 11 were martyred for their faith. Would they have been willing to die for a lie? Would they have been teaching and preaching about Jesus and his message, something that they knew was very likely to eventually lead to their death, if they had not really seen Him after he had arisen?"

Just then, Luke's phone rang. He held up a hand and said "Just one moment". During the very brief phone conversation that ensued, Luke's face took on a look of concern and Dan heard him say "I'll be right there" just before he hung up.

"You will have to excuse me. One of our members has just been taken to the hospital by ambulance. They think he's having a heart attack and"
Dan interrupted.
"I understand. Go ahead. We can finish another time. You have already given me a lot to think about."
Brother Luke quickly thanked Dan and shook his hand before hurrying out the door.

Chapter 17

Ben sat on a bench in front of the offices of Vision Biotech, waiting for Dan to return. He had just re-read the same article three times without comprehending any of it. He was anxious to get his plan set in motion and he had been sitting here for 45 minutes. He supposed that he should have made an appointment but he had no illusions concerning how Dan felt about him and he didn't want to give Dan a chance to side step his attempts to meet.

Now, here Dan came, looking deeply completive and distracted. Oh, and now that he had seen Ben, he looked a bit annoyed. Good thing Ben hadn't tried to make an appointment.

Ben stood and extended his hand as Dan approached. By now, the look of annoyance had disappeared from Dan's face. Dan smiled but it looked a bit forced. He shook Ben's hand and said "Come on in", with little enthusiasm. As they sat across Dan's desk from each other, Dan spoke.

"This is the second time in a week that I have come back to find you just sitting out there. It might be easier on both of us if you would just make an appointment."

Ben just said "I will keep that in mind" and neither of them pursued the subject any further. They sat in uncomfortable silence for a few seconds before Dan said "So, what can I do for you".

"I'm sure you know what I want. I was wondering if you have given any thought to what we discussed last week."

Dan sat for a moment before speaking and appeared to be gathering his thoughts.

"Yes, I have given it a great deal of thought and I have talked to Christine about it but I have not yet talked to Jake. Plus, I do still have some things that I want to think through."

71

"What things? As I said last week, it looks to me like a win-win situation."

"Yes, on the surface, it does. However, and I don't mean to offend, but, given our history, I am having some trouble getting comfortable with this whole thing."

"I can understand that. I want to again assure you that I did not know about the kidnapping of Christine and Jake. I admit that I got overly zealous in my pursuit of the development of this technology and that led me to end up taking any funding that I could get without questioning where it came from or why it was being offered. That was wrong and I'm sorry for the things that you and your family went through as a result. But that same commitment to the technology could serve you very well."

"Yes, possibly."

Dan was proving to be a tougher sell than Ben had anticipated. Ben thought about the letter that he had sent to James Swanson and the letter that he had received, just this morning, in response. Using the information that he had access to, through James, he knew that he could get Dan to bring him on board. Ben wasn't entirely sure that he liked the terms that James had laid out. He still had to think about that. Besides, he didn't want to come on too strong. He didn't want it to appear that he was basically blackmailing Dan into hiring him. That's exactly what he was doing but Dan already had trust issues when it came to Ben and Ben didn't want to exacerbate those trust issues. Doing so would not serve him well later. He decided to take a less direct approach.

"Where are you currently in the process of getting ready to mass produce the implants? I know that's going to be tough. I was dreading getting that set up, when I was still at the helm of the company."

Dan appeared to relax a little. Good. Just one CEO talking shop with the ex-CEO.

"Yes, it is going to be tough. Of course, the whole mess with Biotronics doesn't help any."

"No, it sure doesn't. All in all, I was satisfied with them but I think they were always teetering on the edge of insolvency. We had some project slowdowns that were caused by them not getting components on time because they were not paying the vendors on time. Then, between the bad press that came from James Swanson's involvement in sabotaging Jake's implants and the fact that Vision Biotech was no longer around to prop them up, it just pushed them over the edge."

"Yeah, that's too bad. Larry McDonald, the owner, seems like a really nice guy. Plus, they already sold most of their equipment so we are going to have to front them a truck load of money so they can re-equip. Really, to be fair, we would have had to do that anyway because they could not have mass produced the implants with the equipment they had previously."

"Yes, that equipment will be expensive. When I was running things, we looked at bringing production in house once we got past the clinical trials."

For a few minutes, they talked about the prices of various pieces of equipment from various manufacturers. Ben used the opportunity to demonstrate his knowledge. Dan had probably studied for months just to learn the basics. Ben, on the other hand, could quote every statistic of every machine backward and forward and he knew the ramifications of using one machine over another for a given task. When talking about this stuff, Ben was in his element. Dan appeared to be impressed, which, after all, was the point. Ben decided that the time was right to, gently, set the hook.

"Well, it's probably best that you are continuing to use Biotronics, at least for now, rather than having to deal with the headache of taking everything in house."

Dan nodded.

"You know, there has been a bit of a shakeup over there at Biotronics, what with the mess with James and them almost going out of business. Larry had a group of good guys but they weren't always the best organized. With a project like this, there are reams and reams of data to deal with. With everything that has gone on, I wouldn't be surprised if some data has gotten lost in the shuffle."

A look passed over Dan's face that Ben couldn't read.

"Anyway, I would have duplicates of some of their data in my personal project notes. If I can help, let me know."

There was that look again that Ben couldn't read.

"Sure, I'll do that. Thanks."

"Don't mention it."

Ben got up to leave and the men shook hands.

"Think about it. The way I see it, we need each other and how could I hurt you now anyway? Vinnie Patrillo is in jail and I haven't talked to him in months. I'm not anxious to talk to him either. You and yours aren't the only ones who went through a load of crap because of him. Just think about it.

Chapter 18

Friday morning.

"What! I built this organization! He has no right! I don't care if he is my brother!"

Vinnie Patrillo sat across from Andreas Dizinno. Andreas was Vinnie's attorney and was on the payroll of the Patrillo Crime Family, of which Vinnie was the head. Andreas was more than just Vinnie's attorney. First and foremost, he was also Vinnie's link to the Crime Family, a role to which he was well suited because of the fact that the attorney/client relationship allowed him to meet with Vinnie in private without surveillance. Prison officials knew that Andreas met with Vinnie far more than any other attorney met with any other client within the prison walls. Because of this fact and Vinnie's position within the Patrillo Crime Family, officials knew that Vinnie was continuing to run the organization from his cell, through Andreas, but, lacking any evidence of what communication took place between Vinnie and Andreas, they could not prove it and so were powerless to stop it.

Andreas had just told Vinnie that Vinnie's brother, Antonio, wanted to take over "the business", meaning the Patrillo family organized crime operation.

Cursing loudly, Vinnie repeatedly slammed his hand down onto the plain metal table which sat between he and Andreas and then he got up and began to kick the table repeatedly, hard enough to send it flying were it not bolted to the floor. When he had done this long enough to get a very sore foot, still cursing, he began to pace behind his chair, back and forth, the length of the small room, which was only two strides, giving the whole situation a rather comical look. Andreas just sat and watched in silence, knowing that Vinnie's fury would eventually dissipate enough to allow for rational conversation and knowing that it was pointless to try to talk to him until then.

Eventually, Vinnie stopped pacing and faced Andreas, still standing, with a very red face and hands gripping the back of his chair hard enough for them to shake and his knuckles to turn white. Now, in contrast to all his shouted cursing, he spoke in a very low voice, so quiet that Andreas actually had to strain to hear. He spoke a single word, the single syllable drawn out to cover several seconds.

"Why?"

Andreas was not rattled. He was used to seeing displays of temper from Vinnie like this, though usually not quite so dramatic. He knew that his boss would calm down enough to make a rational plan to deal with the situation but, for now, best to just give him the information and let the drama play out. When Andreas responded, his voice was calm, all business.

"The organization's income is way down."

Vinnie exploded again.

"Way down compared to what? Sure, it's down from a couple years ago but not down from when Pop handed me the rains ten years ago. I've been in here for three months. I have to have time to regroup. I can run things from in here better than Antonio can run them from the outside. Antonio is just jealous. He always has been. He couldn't stand it that Pop wanted me to take over despite that I am the younger brother. Pop knew that Antonio couldn't handle it. Pop was right to hand things over to me then and Antonio still can't handle it now."

When Vinnie paused for a moment, Andreas continued.

"Income is way down but expenditures are not down and the coffers are getting low. Every business that we have is going downhill; prostitution, drugs, loan sharking, money laundering, everything. Some of our top producers are going to work for other organizations. We once supplied over half of the illicit drugs in West Tennessee. Now, our drug volume is down by 20% and our top three pushers are talking about striking out on their own."

"So convince them that they don't need to do that."

"I'm sure we will, eventually, but it won't be easy. Barry was keeping them in line but-"

"and I suppose Antonio blames me for Barry being in here too."

Barry Orsini had been the top enforcer of the Patrillo Crime Family, before he had been put in jail, along with Vinnie, for his part in the kidnaping of Jake and Christine.

"Well, yes, he does blame you for that and a lot of other things. He is raising quite a stink within the organization."

Vinnie had finely calmed down somewhat and he sat in contemplative silence for a few moments before speaking.

"Just a bunch of talk can't hurt me. Action is what matters. Does he have support?"

"Not much, yet, but there is growing unrest with your leadership."

Vinnie was silent for another moment.

"I see. And what does Pop say?"

"You know that your father is a very practical man."

"Just what does that mean?"

"The organization's income has dropped slowly but steadily for the past two years and, since your incarceration, it has dropped sharply."

"What! So are you saying that -"

Andreas kept speaking, at the same conversational volume, and Vinnie stopped talking so that he could hear.

"Your father is a business man, first and foremost. You know that. He is starting to wonder if a change is in order. However, I don't think he is ready to make a change just yet."

Vinnie suddenly looked deflated. He sat with his head hung, looking rather dejected. It was not a look befitting an accomplished and hardened mobster. He sat like that, in total

77

silence, for several minutes, appearing to be in deep thought. Eventually, he spoke, low enough that Andreas had to strain to hear.

"So, how long do I have?"

Andreas couldn't help but feel a little sorry for his boss.

"You ran the organization successfully for a long time. The old man isn't going to kick you out overnight, even if Antonio is insisting on it."

Vinnie smiled at Andreas' use of the name "The Old Man" for Vinnie's father. It was a sort of a term of endearment which some people, such as Andreas, who had been with the family for a long time, used for the patriarch of the crime family.

"I think that The Old Man will give you at least six months to get things back on track. Beyond that, I can't guarantee anything."

Vinnie sat for a few more minutes in contemplative silence. As he did, his mood appeared to improve slightly and, slowly, a slight smile crept across his face.

"Well then, that gives us six months to come up with a plan, doesn't it?"

Andreas said nothing, as nothing was expected, and Vinnie's smile broadened.

"And I think that I already have that plan."

Chapter 19

Friday afternoon, just after lunch, Dan sat at his desk with his head in his hands. He was having a hard time concentrating. He was tired. His week had been very busy, though he had spent the first part of it at home, snowed in. He had spent his time at home productively, most of the time barricaded in his study, working on the plan that he and Mike would eventually present to prospective lenders. Then, back at work on Wednesday, he had begun to do some research into grants which were available for biotech companies, none of which seemed to be suitable for Vision Biotech, certainly none that could be obtained in time to really help with their current problem. Then, on Thursday afternoon, Dan had met with Brother Luke Stanley. To his surprise, Dan just couldn't get that conversation out of his mind. It had even overshadowed the second visit by Ben (Dan hadn't even thought to mention that to Christine yet) and Dan was now again thinking about what Brother Luke had said, almost 24 hours later, as though something kept drawing him back to it. He struggled to focus on work and the problem at hand.

Jake had just had another meeting with David Landers. In light of David's objections, which he had voiced in the previous meeting, and in light of their need to get a capital infusion, Jake had offered to lower the price to seven million. To Jake's surprise, David still wanted to think about it. David had said "as important as this is to me, there are still things that are more important". This had puzzled Jake and, when Jake had reported this to Dan, he was just as puzzled. Dan now sat, pondering this.

His thoughts drifted back to his conversation with Mike Hannon about this. What was it that Mike had said?

"I know David Landers to be a Christian. I have seen his Christian testimony on YouTube. He is a man of strong faith,

faith in Jesus Christ. He understands that there are things much more important than the things of this world, like whether he can see or not. He probably knows that it may not be God's will that he ever see and he is probably at peace with that. In fact, I have heard him say that, in his testimony." Back to this whole issue of faith. Mike has seen David's Christian testimony on YouTube. Hmmm. Testimony. As in to testify. His Christian testimony must be him talking about his life as a Christian, or something like that. Dan thought "Well, if Mike found it on YouTube, I can too" and he reached for his keyboard. He thought that this might help him to understand the situation with David Landers a little better and, at the same time, it also might help him to better understand the things that Brother Luke had said.

In a moment, Dan's computer screen was filled with the image of David Landers, sitting in a chair, wearing his sun glasses and holding a white cane. The image reminded Dan of Jake before he had gained his sight. It also made him ask himself the same question that he had asked himself about Christine and her situation with Roger. If God exists, why would He let someone like this, a seemingly good person, go through all of the hardship that David had endured?

Dan's attention was riveted to the computer as David began to speak. David explained that he had not been born blind but that he had been blinded at a young age, as a result of some eye problems and surgical complications. David told of the hardships that he had endured as a result of his blindness. He told of his educational and employment struggles. He told of the struggles to be taken seriously, by potential employers as well as others. All of this sounded very familiar to Dan as Jake had gone through many of the same things. Dan's attention was fixed even more firmly as David began to talk of the surgeries which took the vision that he had once had.

"When I was 19, I had the surgery that, in the long run, took what little vision that I had. It was not immediately apparent, however, that I would be completely blind as a result of the surgery. At first, the doctors told me that my vision should return. I am a Christian, saved at age 11, and I leaned on God for strength. After all, He had brought me through all of the challenges that I had faced thus far. I prayed for my vision to return but I prayed, above all, for God's will to be done in this situation. Christians often say this but it is one thing to say it and it is quite another to be truly sincere about it. I found that it can be very difficult to say it and really mean it once you figure out that God's will and your own will do not coincide. After three or four months and about as many surgeries, with things getting steadily worse rather than better, it became apparent that my vision was not coming back."

Dan wiped a tear from his eye as he recalled some very similar things that Jake had gone through and his heart went out to David.

"My doctor was renowned as the best retina specialist in the world. He said that the combination of complications that had occurred were, when taken together, almost statistically impossible. I had continually and sincerely prayed that God's will be done in this process. I had the best doctor in the world. And yet, despite all this, what should have been impossible happened. I had to accept the hard conclusion that it was supposed to be this way."

Supposed to be this way? Dan just didn't get it. Rather than helping him to understand, this had only served to deepen his confusion. Based on the things that Brother Luke had said, surely, Jesus really did exist and had done the things that the Bible claimed. And if this was true then surely God did exist as well. But, if God did exist, then why in the world did He allow things like this? David had said that it was supposed to be this way. That sounded to Dan like an empty platitude, perhaps of some comfort to David but with no real meaning. Dan's phone rang. It was Christine. Dan answered and, as he talked, the video continued to go on in the background,

81

making it hard for Dan to hear. He stopped the video. It wasn't like it was helping him anyway. Christine asked Dan to stop at the grocery store to get a few things. He agreed and said that he thought that he was going to head home shortly. "I think that I have run out of gas for this week."

"Come on home. I miss you anyway. I'll make shrimp tacos for supper."

"Oh, please don't."

He was just kidding and she knew it. He loved her cooking and her shrimp tacos were his favorite. They talked on for a few minutes. By the time they hung up, Dan couldn't wait to get home.

He sat for a moment and thought about Christine. She was so wonderful, in so many ways, yet she had gone through and continued to go through so much because of Roger. It just wasn't right and yet God had allowed it. Dan knew that he had to be missing something but he was too tired to think about it just then.

He closed YouTube, shut down the computer, and headed home.

Chapter 20

On Saturday morning, Ben sat at his kitchen table, drinking a cup of coffee and contemplating the letter that sat in front of him. It was not the first time that he had seen the letter. He had received it on Thursday and had read it at least 20 times since then and had even thought about it a great deal more. Much hinged on how Ben responded to the contents.

The letter was from James Swanson. When Ben had begun to read the letter for the first time, he had been elated. It appeared that James could deliver the information that Ben wanted. However, as Ben had continued to read, his enthusiasm waned. He wasn't at all sure that he was comfortable with the price that James had quoted or with the arrangements that he had specified. Yet, he wasn't sure that he really had a choice. It was this which had prompted all the contemplation concerning the letter.

Ben's eyes wondered down to the only paragraph.

"I can indeed deliver the information that you request. You did not name a price that you are willing to pay but you say that you are willing to pay me a fair price for the information, a very subjective term. We cannot negotiate in the abstract. We must deal with concrete numbers and so I will name one. I will take half a million dollars. That number is concrete in more than one sense. It is fixed, non-negotiable. You will deliver a cashier's check, in the stated amount, to my wife, Beth, within 30 days. Upon receipt of said check by her, the information will be delivered to you, within ten days, by a method that I will specify later. The information is not in my house, nor does Beth know where it is, so you cannot simply take it. I eagerly await your decision. A positive decision will be signified by the receipt of the check within the specified time. Similarly, a negative decision will be specified by a lack of receipt of the check, in which case, the information will be destroyed. I sincerely hope that we are able to do business." Ben sat back in deep contemplation, his coffee getting cold. Could he get the money? Yes, it wouldn't be easy but he could. Dan had paid him half a million dollars for his portion of Vision Biotech. Ben had then spent the majority of that money on this house. The purchase of the house had been very recent and the house was in good repair so the house should still be worth as much as Ben had paid for it. He could probably sell it without too much trouble but that would probably take at least a few months and he didn't have time for that. He would have to borrow the money. How could he do that? The house would serve as collateral but, even with adequate collateral, banks don't like to lend money without some evidence of how the borrower would pay it back. At the moment, Ben had no job, though that was hopefully about to change.

This brought Ben to his second point of contemplation. Was this information absolutely necessary to get his foot in the door with Vision Biotech? There was no way to know for sure but Ben thought it probably was. After all, Dan was clearly not excited at the prospect of employing Ben. Ben couldn't blame him, really, but Ben had to get this job if he was to pull off his plan and get back the technology that was, clearly, rightfully his.

Ben was in a bit of a conundrum. He needed money, which he was going to have to borrow, in order to purchase information, which he needed in order to get the job, which he needed in order to borrow the money. He pondered this problem for a moment. He quickly decided that this could be handled easily enough but doing so would require a bit of masterful deception. He may as well get started.

Ben put the letter aside and placed his laptop in front of him. As he waited for it to boot up, he thought everything through once more. He didn't like the circumstances but business was business and you just had to do what you had to do. When the computer was ready, he made a note to call the bank on Monday morning and make an appointment. After thinking about it for a moment, he made a second note to make an appointment with Dan as well. Dan hadn't liked it when Ben had just shown up the last couple times and Ben wanted to keep things cordial, at least for now. With these tasks done, Ben launched a specialized piece of software which he had retained when he had left Vision Biotech.

As Ben waited for the software to load, he finished his now cold coffee. As he thought about the months ahead, Ben smiled. This was going to be fun.

Chapter 21

On Monday afternoon, Dan sat in the reception area of Vision Biotech and waited for the arrival of Ben Nelson, who had called on Monday morning and made an appointment to talk to Dan on Monday afternoon. Dan thought "At least he did make an appointment this time" but Dan was a bit annoyed at having to deal with Ben this afternoon. He wasn't really sure why though. Undoubtedly, Ben wanted to talk about his potential employment with Vision Biotech, a subject that he just wouldn't let go of. Dan and Christine had discussed this very issue over the previous weekend. They had decided that, in light of the fact that Jake was absolutely unwilling to allow the reverse engineering of his implants, they really had no choice but to at least explore the possibility of Ben's employment and whether Ben might be able to offer information that would allow the company to move forward without the reverse engineering. So, Dan had to talk to Ben anyway and the sooner the better. Still, Ben calling to make the appointment had irritated Dan, he supposed because of their history with Ben and Ben's extreme persistence. Oh well. Dan needed to talk to Ben and Ben was coming so, regardless of how that had come about, Dan thought that he may as well make the most of it.

Now, as Dan sat here, waiting for Ben, he tried to decide how to get the information that he wanted without coming right out and asking. It wouldn't do to say "So, Ben, can you please help us to stay in business by giving us this little bit of information that we absolutely must have in order to move forward". No, that wouldn't do at all. Better to appear less than totally desperate. If Dan were to do that, he may as well just go ahead and give Ben the company back. But how should he handle this? He couldn't think of a roundabout way to approach the subject and the whole thing was made more difficult by the fact that they didn't even know for sure that Ben had access to the information that they were seeking. He and Christine had discussed the situation at length but even the normally very resourceful Christine had no practical solution.

Dan had thought about it Sunday morning, while Christine was at church, which is where she had wanted him to be. He didn't want to go with her. Dan couldn't shake his thoughts about what Brother Luke had told him and he supposed that he should make another appointment with Brother Luke to finish the conversation that they had started. On the other hand, Dan also couldn't shake the thought that there was something that just wasn't right about the situation with Christine and Roger and about the things that had been revealed in the portion of David Landers' testimony that Dan had watched. Dan was torn. He wanted to get to know God and, at the same time, he wasn't sure that he wanted to know God. He couldn't reconcile his feelings so he just did his best to ignore them. He couldn't do that very well at church so he begged off going, something that Christine had become accustomed to anyway and so thought little of it. Dan spent two hours, while Christine was at church, playing various scenarios in his mind, and nothing seemed to work well. Well, it was almost time for Ben to arrive and Dan had nothing. He supposed that he would just have to wing it. In all fairness, Dan hadn't expected to meet with Ben quite this soon but it didn't really matter as he didn't think that he would have come up with anything even if he had another week. Oh well, it would work out, somehow. Things always did.

Just then, there was a knock on the front door. Ben stuck his head in and said "knock knock".

Dan put on a smile that he hoped looked more genuine than it felt.

"Come on in. Want some coffee? I just made some fresh."

"No thanks. I'm good."

Dan ushered Ben into his office where they quickly settled in.

"I asked for this meeting so I guess I'll start."

"OK. Fair enough."

"I know that you are missing some of the records pertaining to the implants, specifically pertaining to the tertiary optical transducer."

Dan's mouth fell open and a look of astonishment came over his face. The look of astonishment was quickly replaced by a look of suspicion and accusation.

"Now Dan, don't look at me like that. I assure you that I had nothing to do with the information having gone missing. I told you that the good folks over at Biotronics were never the most organized. I'm sure that the missing information that I just mentioned simply fell victim to that lack of organization. Come on, Dan. Don't be so suspicious."

The look on Dan's face softened somewhat and, after just a second or two of silence, he spoke.

"Ben, please don't take this the wrong way but you must forgive me if I don't have absolute trust in you, especially after our history and when you waltz in here and make an announcement like that."

"Oh, I understand entirely and I do forgive you. In fact, there is nothing to forgive. I am hopeful that I can re-establish the bond of trust between us."

Dan thought "Re-establish, what do you mean re" but he said nothing.

Ben reached into his pocket and pulled out a USB flash drive, which he dropped in the middle of Dan's desk. Dan slowly reached out and picked it up.

"What's this?"

"That is the missing information on the tertiary optical transducer."

Dan's mouth again fell open and, this time, he didn't know what to say and, after several seconds, Ben spoke.

"It's yours. I mean, it's rightfully yours anyway but now you have possession of it."

"But how did you -"

"It doesn't really matter how I got it, does it?"

"It just might".

Ben shook his head.

"Dan, Dan, Dan. Always so suspicious. OK, if you must know, I kept copies of all of our internal project notes as well as all of the project notes from Biotronics. With everything being filed electronically, it was very easy to do. Shortly before the unfortunate incident involving the Patrillos -"

"Unfortunate incident?"

"Shortly before the unfortunate incident involving the Patrillos, while reviewing our data, I found that this information concerning the tertiary optical transducer was missing. I wasn't concerned because the information was also present in my personal project notes. I had previously copied it to be used in conjunction with some work that I was doing at home one evening. Anyway, apparently, after I had copied the information, someone at Biotronics accidentally deleted the information from the official project record. Before I had a chance to copy the data from my notes back to the official record, everything blew up and, suddenly, a little missing data was the least of my concerns."

"That was months ago. Why bring me the information now."

"I just recently again thought about it, probably prompted by all of our recent interaction, and I thought what better way to gain your trust than to give you the information freely."

"Simply out of the goodness of your heart?"

"Sure. Why not? Like I said, it's rightfully yours anyway."

"I'm sure that there is a quid pro quo here. What do you want?"

"All I want is your good will."

With that and without another word, Ben rose and quickly left the building, leaving Dan sitting there, with his mouth open and the flash drive in his hand.

Chapter 22

That evening, Christine sat at her kitchen table, with Dan on one side and Jake on the other. In front of them was a meal of fried catfish, hush puppies, baked potatoes, and cold slaw. Lately, things had been a bit tense between Dan and Jake, ever since the issues had come up related to the missing data about the implants and Jake's absolute refusal to undergo the reverse engineering procedure. This dinner was Christine's attempt to get the brothers together in a relaxed atmosphere where they could either talk things out or at least start to move on and just let some of the tension dissipate. The whole time she had been cooking, she had also been praying and, so far, things were going well, much to her relief.

The food was delicious and conversation was very light hearted. At the moment, Dan and Jake were talking about Jake's new truck.

"Every time I pass the darned thing, I want to jump in and drive to Memphis, or Nashville, or maybe both."

Everyone laughed.

"When I bought it for you, I didn't think about how not yet being able to drive it would drive you crazy. We are going to have to get started with driving lessons."

"You're telling me!"

"I'll tell you what. Tomorrow, when I come to pick you up for work, I will leave my truck at your house and we will take your truck. We have that huge back lot at the office. We can spend our lunch break driving around back there. In the meantime, start looking into what you have to do to get a learner's permit so that we can get you out on the road."

"Sounds great!"

Christine smiled. She was glad to see tensions easing between the two brothers.

Jake opened his mouth to say something else but Dan, who had just put a huge bite of fish in his mouth, held his hand up to prevent Jake from speaking while Dan chewed. When Dan finished, he wiped his mouth and sat back with a huge grin on his face.

"I have something that you may like as much as starting driving lessons."

"That isn't possible."

"Don't count on it."

"OK, what is it?"

Dan reached into his pocket and pulled out a small object which he then placed in the center of the table with a flourish. Christine and Jake both stared at it for a moment before Jake grabbed it and held it high above his head.

"How did you know, just what I always wanted, a USB flash drive!"

Christine laughed.

"Ever the comedian, aren't you, Einstein?"

"Well I do try."

"And you do an excellent job too but I have a feeling that it is what is on the flash drive that Dan thinks will excite you."

"Perhaps, but he has not yet seen fit to tell me what that is."

"Yes, that is an excellent point."

They both looked at Dan.

"Why is it that the two of you always team up against me? Well, it doesn't matter. Even your combined efforts cannot dampen my mood this fine evening."

"If you don't hurry up and tell us what is on that thing, when we do our driving lesson, I am going to wreck your side of the truck."

"You wouldn't dare wreck your own new and shiny truck, even to get back at me, but I will go ahead and tell you anyway. On this drive, sir and madam, is the formerly missing data concerning the tertiary optical transducer."

Christine's and Jake's mouths fell open. They looked much the same way that Dan had looked after first hearing the news. Jake was first to recover and speak.

"So this means that, even with me not undergoing the reverse engineering procedure, everything can still go forward?"

"That is correct."

Jake looked absolutely ecstatic. By now, Christine had sufficiently recovered enough to speak. She placed her hand on Dan's arm as she spoke.

"That's wonderful but where in the world did you get it?"

"Ben Nelson."

"But how -"

"This morning, he called and made an appointment to see me this afternoon. When he showed up, he gave me this."

"In exchange for what?"

"Nothing."

"Nothing?"

"He says that he only wants our goodwill."

Christine and Jake spoke simultaneously.

"Bologna!"

"Yes, I agree, but that's what he says and, regardless of his true motives, we now have the information."

Jake stood and started excitedly pacing.

"This is great. I felt so bad at having let you down, Dan, and having let down all those who would potentially benefit from the technology. Still, I just couldn't go through with the reverse engineering procedure and the potential risks, minimal as they might be. Now, it's OK. We have the information anyway and it was much faster and much easier this way."

After a moment, during which Jake continued his pacing, Dan spoke.

"I will admit that I may have been somewhat disappointed but I don't think that anyone really blamed you for feeling the way that you did and, as you said, we now have the information and it is much easier this way."

Christine was excited but also troubled and it was she who next spoke.

"Maybe it's too easy."

Dan and Jake both looked at her.

"What do you mean?"

"We don't know what Ben's motives are and his true motives do matter, don't they? I mean think about it. Think about our history with Ben. Does he seem like someone who would do something like this, just out of the goodness of his heart, expecting nothing in return?"

Dan and Jake continued to look at her but neither of them spoke. After a moment, she continued.

"I guarantee you that he wants something more than just our goodwill and we had better figure out what that something is. It may be something that we aren't willing to give."

Dan said "He probably just wants that job that he keeps bugging me about".

Christine said "Yes, probably, but why does he want it so badly".

Jake said "Maybe he just wants to break back into the biotech field and keep working with the technology that he developed".

Dan nodded but Christine shook her head.

"No, I think it's more than just that. He has been so aggressively persistent. Giving us this information seams out of character for him and is probably motivated by his desire to get this job. He seems desperate to get it. If he is that desperate then there is a reason. What is it? I'm telling you, we had better be careful here."

A somewhat uncomfortable silence fell and everyone picked at their food. Christine felt bad at having spoiled the festive mood. She wondered if she was being the voice of reason or the voice of paranoia. Perhaps she needed to work on forgiving Ben just like she needed to work on forgiving Roger. On the other hand, even forgiveness didn't mean ignoring a person's negative character traits, did it? Even Christians had to use a certain amount of prudence, a certain amount of diligence, when dealing with other people, especially people who had proven themselves to be untrustworthy in the past. Christians were to be forgiving but the word Christian wasn't Greek for "door mat". She felt very conflicted. Was this conflict just her mixed up emotions or was it conflict between her own spirit and the Holy Spirit, trying to convict her about her attitude. She needed to do some sewing, some thinking, and some praying.

After a few more minutes of relative silence, Christine cleared the dishes and left the men in the living room, talking over fresh coffee, while she disappeared back into her sewing room.

Chapter 23

Christine sat down at her sewing table and looked around the room. She loved this room, which she used for not only sewing but also reading and just relaxing. It was very cozy. Besides her sewing table and cabinet containing various sewing notions, there were two overstuffed chairs, one of which had a stack of fabric samples in it and there were several articles of clothing which were awaiting alterations draped over one arm. These chairs sat in front of built in book cases which flanked a small fireplace.

Christine loved a fire in the winter. This house had four fireplaces, one in the living room, one in the master bedroom, one in Dan's study, and one in this room. The many fireplaces were one of the things that she loved about the house. As she stared straight ahead at the unlit gas logs, she decided that a nice fire might brighten her mood a little. It certainly couldn't hurt anyway.

On her way back from lighting the fire, she noticed her Bible, which was laying in one of the overstuffed chairs, where she had her quiet time and had done her Bible study this morning. She stopped and looked down at the open Bible, which was open to Psalm 46:10, which had been the focal scripture of her Bible Study this morning.

As she stood there, looking down at the Bible, she read "Be still, and know that I am God". There was a little more to the passage but she stopped right there because she was gripped with a sudden and powerful conviction to do exactly what she had just read. She fell to her knees in front of the chair. She pushed the Bible toward the back of the chair as she rested her head on the front. Earnestly, she prayed.

"God, I want to be still before You right now, to acknowledge Your awesome power and Your eternal goodness, to rest in Your sovereignty and Your saving grace. I feel You strongly

99

impressing on my heart that I need to pray right now. I want to be obedient but I don't know what it is that I am supposed to pray for."

Although she didn't know what she was supposed to pray about, she assumed that it had something to do with the situation with Ben and her forgiveness or lack of it and maybe even the situation with Roger too. As she prayed, she poured her heart out before God, telling Him of her confusion and her feelings of inadequacy. She told Him of her desire to exhibit Christ like forgiveness but also to exhibit strength in the face of potential threats to herself and those she loved. As she prayed for God's guidance, she felt that He had something specific that He wanted to convey to her in this moment. She prayed for discernment to recognize exactly what He was trying to tell her.

"Hire him."

Hire who? Ben? Where had that thought come from? Was it God? It certainly wasn't Christine herself. She didn't think she wanted anything to do with Ben and she didn't want Dan or Jake to either.

"Hire him."

Christine didn't think that this made any sense and she told God so.

"God, do you want me to ask Dan to hire Ben? I don't understand. I am almost sure that Ben is not a Christian. Of course, even if he is not a Christian, you could still use him in order to accomplish your -"

"Hire him."

"But God, I know that Ben says that he didn't have anything to do with kidnapping me and Jake, and of course you know if he did or didn't but he was definitely associated with the Petrillos and so he might -"

"Hire him."

"You know that I have really struggled with forgiveness lately. I have sought Your guidance but I have still struggled. Are you trying to teach me a lesson about that?"

She sensed no response.

"God?"

Though she did still feel God's presence, again, she sensed no response from Him. She had clearly gotten the message that she was to ask Dan to hire Ben. However, still, she sought some sort of clarification or explanation. Apparently, none was to be forthcoming. Brother Luke had said that God often expects obedience even without understanding, in other words, faith. Christine knew that this was true but, still, it was hard. Never the less, she strove to be obedient. Having discerned God's will, her prayers now centered on asking God to give her the strength to carry out that will, even though she didn't understand it.

When she was done, she felt a sense of peace descend on her, despite no better understanding than when she had walked into the room. There was a certain peace that came from just knowing that she was abiding in God's will and that made her smile.

As she rose to her feet, her eyes fell on the Bible that she had pushed to the back of the chair, having closed it as she had done so. She felt a compulsion to open it again. When she did, her eyes fell on Romans 8:28.

"And we know that all things work together for good to those who love God, to those who are the called according to His purpose"

She smiled again. She thought "Well, God, I love you and I am doing my best to seek your purpose so I am going to trust You on this".

With that, she left the room with a confident and purposeful stride to go tell Dan and Jake.

Chapter 24

Two months later. Thursday, the day before Good Friday.
Ben Nelson sat at his desk at Vision Biotech and thought back
over his first two months with the company. The experience
had definitely been interesting.

There had been the matter of Ben's office. The building in
which Vision Biotech currently resided was very small. There
was a small reception area, two offices, a kitchen, and a
bathroom. That was it. When Ben had come, Dan occupied
one office and Jake occupied the other. Ben had hoped that
they would put him in Jake's office and move Jake somewhere
else. This was not to be, however, and so Ben found himself
occupying the reception area. Though it did serve the
intended purpose, it was smaller than either Dan's or Jake's
work spaces and it afforded little privacy. Ben felt that it was
beneath him. He was, after all, the man who had started this
company and he was mostly responsible for developing the
company's technology. Oh well, Ben knew that he would be
back behind Dan's desk soon enough and, besides, the
company was going to have to move to larger facilities very
soon anyway and he was sure that he would get a bigger and
better office then.

With Ben's contributions, things were moving along very
rapidly. Within six months, in Ben's estimation, the company
would again be ready to begin performing implantation
procedures. Both Dan and Jake were elated and Ben's stock
appeared to be rising in their eyes. After the meeting, back in
February, during which Ben had given the information to Dan,
Ben had been unsure about his chances for getting on board.
However, Dan had called him the very next day and asked
when he could start. Initially, Dan and Jake were nice enough
but a bit reserved and, really, who could blame them. Now,
though, two months later, with Ben having made several

positive contributions and having done nothing underhanded, that they knew about, Dan and Jake were both really warming up to Ben. They might even be beginning to trust him. All in all, things were going even better than Ben had expected.

Ben's thoughts were interrupted by Dan speaking as he passed by.

"See you Monday Ben. Happy Easter."

Ben just smiled and waved as Dan disappeared out the front door.

Ben looked at the clock on his computer screen. It was 2:30. The office was going to be closed tomorrow for Good Friday and Ben had known that Dan planned to leave early today but he hadn't expected him to leave quite this early. So much the better. Ben had to take care of something covertly and so he needed everyone out of the building. Lately, it seemed like either Dan or Jake was always there. Jake had not come in today and now Dan had left very early. This was the perfect opportunity for Ben to do what he had to do. He stood and went to look out of the front window. He wanted to make sure that Dan's truck was gone, which it was. Perfect.

As he went back to his desk, he pulled a USB flash drive out of his pocket. He sat down and inserted it into the computer. Once the computer recognized the drive, he began to copy files from it, replacing files on the main server. He actually could have probably done this when Dan and Jake were here but both of them often walked through the reception area, either talking to Ben or going back and forth between each other's offices and he didn't want one of them to notice what he was doing. His task was made easier by the fact that he had recently convinced them that all project material should be kept on the main server, in order to better facilitate easier access to all materials by everyone and in order to simplify the process of backing up the data. What he hadn't told them was that it also made it easier for him to replace project files by using his own computer so that he wouldn't have to take the chance of getting caught at one of their desks.

When Ben had given Dan the USB flash drive with the information about the tertiary optical transducer, it had not been the real information because, at the time, Ben did not yet have the information. It took a little time to borrow the money, to pay James off, and to get the information from Beth. However, Ben had not wanted to wait that long and so he had simply used his expertise concerning the design of the implants to make up some design schematics and specifications which looked convincing enough to fool Dan. Ben was glad that he had done this. He was convinced that this little gesture of good will on his part was what had gotten him this job. Giving them the information before he actually had it had allowed him to get this job sooner than he otherwise would have and, because of this, he was already in the good graces of the Richardsons. Now, he had to replace the information that he had previously given to Dan with the real information. Creation of the new implants would start soon and it wouldn't do for design of those implants to be guided by faulty data. After all, ultimately, Ben wanted this technology to succeed. He just wanted to derail it for a while. With the procedure finished, Ben removed the flash drive. He smiled as he thought about how easy the Richardsons had proven to be to manipulate thus far.

Chapter 25

Early on the morning of Good Friday, Dan sat at the desk in his study. He had awakened early and, unable to get back to sleep, he had gotten up so that his tossing and turning wouldn't wake Christine. Later that day, they were to go to Emmanuel Baptist Church and help to get things set up for the Easter program that was to be held this upcoming Easter Sunday. There would be a dramatic presentation done by the children and youth, then a time of special music by the choir and several soloists, and then an Easter message by Brother Luke which, it had been promised, had the potential to be life changing. Christine had talked Dan into going on Sunday and she had even talked him into helping out today with setting everything up. Setting up was to be an all-day project and he would have to start getting ready before long but, for now, he sat here, deep in thought.

The last couple months had gone very well. Dan had received the information from Ben, whom Dan had then hired, at Christine's request, and Ben's employment with the company had worked out very well thus far. It looked like the company would be ready to again begin implantation procedures in six months and that was, in large part, thanks to Ben.

Dan had Christine to thank for having hired Ben. Though she clearly didn't like Ben, Christine had claimed that she had felt led of the Holy Spirit to ask Dan to hire him. Dan had been surprised at this request and he had been a bit taken aback by it. After all, though Dan hadn't been quite as suspicious of Ben as Christine had been, Dan didn't really like Ben or completely trust him either. Dan was struck by Christine's commitment to do what she thought that God wanted, even when it was not what she wanted. Dan still wasn't sure about this whole "led by the Holy Spirit" thing but he had to admit that she was always praying and she did seem to have uncommonly good judgment. He had begun to wonder if these two things were possibly connected in some way. In the end, it was his respect for Christine and her judgment that had prompted Dan to hire Ben, a decision that was, by all indications, working out very well.

Perhaps this should have pushed Dan one step closer to faith. In a way, it did, but all that he really felt at the moment was an increase in his confusion concerning God. Dan thought back to his conversation with Brother Luke. Dan had never followed up to finish that conversation but, based on what Brother Luke had said, surely, God really did exist. Surely, Jesus had really lived and done the things that the Bible claimed. Obviously, Christine did believe in God and cared deeply about what He wanted, even when God's wishes conflicted with her own and when His ways were beyond her understanding. Surely, God did love Christine, and yet, He had allowed the things that she had gone through with Roger and He had allowed those things to continue to cast a shadow over her life, even now. That didn't sound much like love to Dan.

What about Jake? As far as Dan knew, Jake was not a Christian. He was a really good person though and, though Jake did have perfect eyesight now, he had gone through years of hardship as a result of his blindness. Why? Did God require that one be in His Christian club in order to curry His favor? Besides, Christine was a Christian and what good had that done her? Dan was very confused.

Thinking about Jake reminded Dan of David Landers. Like Christine, David was a Christian. Not only that but he was a Christian who had apparently dedicated his career and even his life to the things of God. From watching David's Christian testimony on YouTube, Dan knew that, Like Jake, David had gone through a great deal of hardship because of his blindness. God had apparently seen fit to allow it, and yet, this didn't seem to dampen David's love for God or his

108

dedication to Him in the slightest. What had David said about
the complications that had led to his blindness?
"What should have been impossible happened. I had to accept
the hard conclusion that it was supposed to be this way."
Supposed to be this way? Dan shook his head. He just didn't
get it. Thinking about David's testimony deepened Dan's
confusion but it also piqued his curiosity. He thought "I have
got to finish watching that testimony".
Just then, Dan heard Christine walking down the hall. He
looked at the clock. It was 7 am. Gee-whiz! Where had the
time gone? He had better get going. He jumped up and
headed to take a shower.

Chapter 26

At 7:30 am, outside Dan's and Christine's house, a white Chevrolet Impala slowed slightly as it passed by. At 4 pm, the previous afternoon, a black Chevrolet Silverado had passed by. In the past week, several similarly nondescript vehicles had passed by the house, at various times of the day. None had passed by between the hours of 10 pm and 6 am, as the driver of all these vehicles, who was the same man in each case, did not wish to be seen by the guard who was always on duty during those hours. The man knew of the guards and a great deal of other things as well, because of a vast network of resources which was available to him. The man didn't think that the guards would recognize him but, in his line of work, one could never be too careful. He knew that neither Dan nor Christine would recognize him, even if they were to see him, because they had never seen him before. However, he had seen them many times and, before it was all over, they would see him. He had a score to settle.

Steve Levet did not think of himself as a vengeful man. He generally did not dwell on failures. This was not because of some sort of superior life philosophy. It was simply because he generally did not fail. In fact, this had been his first time and he was not taking it well.

Steve Levitt was a "fixer" who worked for the health insurance industry. The failure which had made Steve so bitter had begun before the clinical trial of the artificial retinal implants which had given Jake Richardson his eyesight. The health insurance industry hadn't been happy about all of the money that they were about to have to pay out on behalf of thousands of blind people, in the event of a successful clinical trial of the implants. So, the industry had set out, through Steve, to make sure that the first clinical trial was not a success. Steve had found James, who, at the time, had been the head lab tech at

Biotronics, the company which had manufactured the implants. James had helped to oversee the project and so he had a great deal of knowledge concerning the inner workings of the implants. Steve had caught James at a particularly low point, financially, and had offered him money to sabotage the left implant by reprograming it. The plan was thwarted when Jake had accidentally discovered the reprogramming before the implant was activated.

Ultimately, though the general availability of the technology had been slowed somewhat, it looked like things were quickly getting back on track. Even the slowing of the technological development hadn't been really due to anything that Steve had done. It had been mostly because of the scandal that had resulted when the connection was uncovered between Vision Biotech and the Patrillo Crime Family and the related money laundering operation. All Steve had done was expose himself to risk with no real gain.

Speaking of risk, Steve was concerned about the situation with James. James had been caught before he had received any of the money, other than a very small advance, and now he sat in jail with a ten year sentence, more broke than ever, and with a wife who, according to Steve's sources, was threatening to leave him. In other words, James was a desperate man and desperate men could be dangerous. James knew who Steve was and he just might be willing to talk in exchange for money or a shortened sentence, if the opportunity were to present itself. So, Steve had to make it so that it was worth more to James to remain silent.

However, dealing with James was to be just the beginning. Steve was a man unaccustomed to failure and he had been called on the carpet for this one, something to which he was also unaccustomed and which he didn't like. Those who funded Steve's work had thought that they had the right to expect more from a man who was paid five million dollars per year and they had plainly told him so. Though Steve had

112

always previously worked with complete autonomy, his employers now expected regular and detailed updates concerning his progress. Steve was a man who liked to be in charge and who liked to be feared. This little fiasco had cost him both power and respect and someone was going to pay for that.

Also, Steve knew that his livelihood depended on the recovery of his professional reputation. He had been known as a man who was expensive but worth it because he always got results, until now. In this case, he had not gotten results, not the first time anyway. Now, he intended to erase this blot on his previously perfect record. He intended to get results and he knew how he was going to do it.

He looked at himself in the mirror and smiled. It was now time to put his plan into motion.

Chapter 27

Dan sat at a table in the fellowship hall of Emmanuel Baptist Church, drinking a glass of iced tea and fanning himself. He was in pretty good shape, for a man of his age, but he hadn't worked this hard in a long time. He had just helped to construct the set that was to be used for the children's program. He had then helped to entirely rearrange the fellowship hall and set up additional tables and chairs. This was done in order to accommodate the very large crowd that was expected for the Easter lunch that was to be hosted by the church, after the service on Sunday. Now, he and a few other people were scattered throughout the fellowship hall, resting and awaiting the next task.

There were a couple small groups who were engaged in light conversation. It appeared that everyone was too tired to talk animatedly. Other than Dan, there was one other loaner, sitting several feet away. Dan started to go over and try to talk to the man but then Dan noticed him thumbing through a Bible. Dan didn't really want to get into a conversation about the Bible or anything concerning his relationship with God so he decided to leave the man alone and just rest for a few minutes in solitude.

After a few minutes, Dan became bored. He got out his iPad and started browsing news articles. There wasn't much in the news that was of any real interest and he quickly became bored again. He looked over at the man with the Bible and he again thought back to the Christian testimony of David Landers, which he had begun to watch on YouTube and which he had been meaning to finish. He thought "well, no time like the present".

He got out his ear buds, so as not to disturb anyone, and he launched the YouTube app. He quickly found David's testimony. It took a few minutes to find the exact spot where he had left off watching previously. He knew that he had found the spot when he heard David say "I had to accept the hard conclusion that it was supposed to be this way", the phrase that had so perplexed Dan ever since he had heard David say it when he had first watched the video. Dan thought "Maybe I'll begin to understand" and, though he wasn't at all hopeful about that, he let the video play.

"The last time that I saw anything was on the morning of January 6, 1997. That was 18 years ago and, in those intervening 18 years, I have faced many trials and tribulations as a result, much more even than I have spoken of here. And how about the almost 20 years of my life that came before that? As I have explained, having 20/500 vision is no picnic either and I endured no small amount of heartache in those years. Why did all of that happen to me? I have been a Christian since age 11 and, though I certainly am not perfect, I have, for the most part, done my best to do what I thought that God expected of me. So, why were those 38 years of adversity necessary?"

Dan thought "Yes, exactly, that's what I want to know". The video continued to play and all of Dan's attention was captured by it.

"First, the whole experience has brought me closer to Christ. In many of my trials, I have had to lean on God just to get through the situation. In times of tribulation, I pray more and I get into the Word more and that's how you get close to Christ. Of course, I should do that all of the time but, let's face it, most Christians do better about that in times of tribulation. The Bible says, in Psalm 119:67, 'Before I was afflicted I went astray, but now I keep Your word'. Ecclesiastes 7:3 says 'Sorrow is better than laughter, for by a sad countenance the heart is made better'. It is most often in the hard times that I grow as a Christian but it's hard to think about that in the middle of the hard times. Think about something. When my kids are sick or hurt, how do they know that they can come to

116

me and I will help them? They know that I should because I am their parent but how do they know that I really will? They know from experience, because I have done it before. How do we know that our Heavenly Father will help us through our tribulation? It says so in His Word but, sometimes, that isn't enough for us. As we face storms and He helps us through them, He proves Himself to us. We know that He will help us through the storms because He has always been faithful before and He always will be. Romans 5:3-4 says that tribulation produces perseverance; and perseverance, character; and character, hope. We can always have hope because He will never leave us alone in the middle of a storm."

Hmmm. Dan hadn't thought about it in quite that way before. He thought about Christine. God had allowed all of the things that she had gone through with Roger but He had brought her safely through it. One of the things that Dan had always admired about her, one of the things that set her apart, was her quiet strength, her constant hope that seemed to be independent of her circumstances. Had her tribulation related to her relationship with Roger been at least partly responsible for that strength and that hope? David seemed to be saying that, ultimately, this hope came from God. Was that where Christine's hope came from?

Dan was more engrossed than ever and the video continued. "Speaking of hope, here is the other reason for my tribulation. I am able to testify to Christ's role in my life and how He has helped me to bear up against adversity. The Bible says, in 1 Peter 3:15, 'always be ready to give a defense to everyone who asks you a reason for the hope that is in you'. We are to explain the reason for our hope to those who ask. But, why would they ask? I do OK now but my financial success is relatively recent. For a long time, I really struggled, mostly because of my blindness and, even now, I face a lot of non-financial struggles because of it. What if it wasn't this way? What if I had always had normal vision. What if I had gotten a job as an executive with some big company, making $200K per year, with two trophy houses, four shiny cars, and a boat? Would many people have asked me the reason for the hope that was within me? Probably not. In that circumstance, most people would have assumed that any hope that I outwardly displayed was a result of all of my worldly success. What about the way that it did happen? Many of the hardships that I have gone through have led people to ask how I do it. Because they asked, I could tell them. Because they asked, they actually wanted to hear the answer. Many of these people, if they had not asked, if I had just started talking, they would not have listened. That, too, is why all the tribulation was necessary."

Dan now thought about Jake. He thought about how Jake's previous circumstances could give him a platform which he could use to speak to others about their own struggles and to encourage them. But Jake didn't seem to have the same peace that David had. After all, Jake had been panicked at just the thought of the very small possibility of losing the vision which he had recently gained. Of course, if what Dan had begun to suspect was true, that Christine's and maybe David's hope came from a relationship with God, then Jake wouldn't have the same hope that they had because Jake was not a Christian. Dan was not a Christian either but maybe it was time to think a little more seriously about that, to think about it on more than just an intellectual level.

Dan was startled when someone clapped him on the shoulder. He jumped and turned to see the man with the Bible.

"Oh, I'm sorry. I didn't mean to startle you."

"No problem. I was lost in my own world, watching this video."

"That's David Landers. We had him in concert here a couple years ago. He has a heck of a voice on him. He has an amazing testimony too."

"Yeah, I was just watching his testimony. His story is incredible and his attitude is really amazing too."

"Well, I didn't mean to interrupt you. Go right ahead."

The man turned to go and then quickly turned back and put his hand on Dan's shoulder.

"You will be here on Sunday, won't you?"

"Oh, yes, I wouldn't miss it."

As the man walked away, Dan reflected on what he had just said and he was surprised to find that he actually meant it.

Chapter 28

On Saturday morning, not long after breakfast, James Swanson was told that he had a visitor. He assumed that it was Beth. Her visits had become less frequent and, as far as he knew, she hadn't planned to come this weekend. Then again, it had been very pretty outside, from what he could tell from his occasional short visits to the exercise yard, and he knew that Beth loved the Spring. Perhaps this had lightened her mood and she had decided to make an unannounced visit. She had seemed somewhat warmer toward him since receiving the money from Ben. When James had initially contacted her and told her of the situation and the part that he would need her to play, she had seemed very reluctant. She had become much more willing when she had found out that they stood to gain half a million dollars. She had found the files, right where James had told her that they would be and she had then, upon receipt of payment, transferred the files to Ben. The money would allow her and the kids to make it without struggling until James could get out of here. So, just maybe, she would wait for him.

James was lost in his thoughts and so he did not initially notice when the guard marched him right past the corridor that led to the common visiting room, where he and Beth had always visited. He didn't notice until they approached a metal door that James had been through only once before, when he had met with his attorney, Charles Lawson, to discuss a possible appeal. James was confused.

"Why are you taking me in here?"

"This is where all the meetings with attorneys are held for this cell block."

"But I'm not meeting with my attorney."

"I guess you and your attorney are going to have to coordinate schedules better, which shouldn't be hard for you considering that your schedule is the same every day."

James was still puzzled and not amused. Why would Mark meet with him, unannounced, on a Saturday?

The guard opened the door and James started speaking before he had fully come through it.

"Hey Charles, I don't know why -"

James stopped speaking and moving as Steve Levet reached across the small metal table to shake his hand.

"Hi James. I'm Steve, one of Charles' partners. Charles couldn't make it today and so he sent me. I have been fully briefed on everything concerning your case. There is an important matter that we need to discuss.

James was stunned. He had never expected to see Steve again. He was finally able to reach out and shake Steve's hand but he still couldn't find his voice.

After just a few seconds, the guard left. Not long after that, James found his voice.

"What the crap are you doing here?"

Steve smiled.

"Not glad to see me?"

"Not exactly. And, now that I think about it, how did you arrange to meet with me like this. You aren't my attorney and you aren't one of his partners either!"

"No, I'm not, but the prison's computer doesn't know that. Computers are very gullible. They tend to believe whatever you tell them. Among my various resources, I have people who are very good at making computers believe things. If they think that I am your attorney then we can meet privately and so we can discuss whatever we want."

"As far as I am concerned, we don't have anything to discuss. Trying to pull off your little stunt got me thrown in here and I didn't get anything for it, other than the little advance that you gave me."

122

"Little advance? As I recall, you didn't think that it was so little at the time I gave it to you."

"At the time, I didn't know that was all I was going to get for doing something that was going to land me in jail for ten years. I got what, a couple thousand? Not exactly worth it."

"You are right. It isn't worth it. So, I am here to offer you more."

"Why. I am in jail. I can't help you now. Of course, you know that."

"No, you can't help me."

"Well, I'm sure that you aren't going to pay me just so you don't have so much money to keep track of and invest. Get to it. What do you want from me?"

"You are correct when you said that you can't help me. However, you can hurt me. You not doing that is worth something to me."

Suddenly, it dawned on James. He was the only one who knew that it was Steve who was behind the sabotage attempt. At this realization, he felt a curious mix of emotions. He was exhilarated at the thought that he had something that he could hold over Steve's head. This could be worth a lot of money. On the other hand, he was terrified at the thought that he had something that he could hold over Steve's head. With his resources, Steve could undoubtedly be a dangerous man and he probably didn't like having things held over his head. Well, Steve was offering money so, apparently, he wasn't contemplating any unpleasant options at the moment. James figured that, if he wanted to keep it that way, he had better play along.

"I see where you are coming from here. Exactly how much is my silence worth to you?"

"I figure that half a million should do it. That's fifty thousand for each year that you are in here, which, as I recall, is more than you were making on the outside."

James couldn't believe his luck. Half a million from Ben and half a million from Steve. A million dollars. James was going to get rich, just sitting in jail. He still couldn't help but be a bit nervous about his own safety though, not to mention the safety of Beth and the kids. He decided that it would be wise to try to offer Steve something of value, other than just his silence, which Steve could obtain in ways other than bribery. "You know, Steve, the artificial retina project is getting back on track."

Steve's expression turned icy.

"Yes, I know. My sources tell me that they will be ready to again begin implantation procedures in about six months." James hadn't known that things were proceeding quite so quickly. His little contribution must have really helped out. He had to be careful here. Steve didn't need to know about that little contribution.

"Six months? Really?"

"That's what I'm told."

"As the desired end result was not obtained last time, I'm sure you will try again. Perhaps I could again help you with that?"

"I notice that you made no mention of why the desired result was not obtained last time."

James had feared this. Apparently Steve at least partially blamed him for the failure to stop the project in the previous attempt, which was all the more reason that James should fear him.

"That wasn't my fault."

"Oh?"

"The software that Jake used to access the implants, which gave him the warning about the voltage, was a later version of the software that I used. My software gave no such warning. That software was developed internally by Vision Biotech, not by my company, so how was I to know that they were running a version of the software internally that was later than the version that I had?"

Steve appeared to consider this for a moment. Then, he appeared to relax, somewhat.

"OK, fair enough, but how do you intend to help me? You, yourself, just said that there is nothing that you can do to help me from in here."

"Yes, I did say that, but perhaps I was being a bit short sighted. I hadn't considered all the possibilities."

"OK, I'm listening."

"Perhaps we could have some meetings about my legal defense. It is a very complicated defense and so it will require meeting frequently and for long periods of time. You will have a lot of files that you will need to access with a computer, a computer that my wife, Beth, will supply to you."

Steve had relaxed entirely now and he looked intrigued.

"If you have access to this computer, then you can formulate a plan which will allow me to stop the project from going forward?"

"I believe so."

Steve appeared deep in thought for a moment.

"And exactly what would you require as payment for this service?"

"Nothing."

"Nothing? Oh, come now. I am not a fool."

"No, of course you are not. That is why I am doing this. As a very astute man, you surely realize that you can simply have me eliminated in order to insure my silence. As another astute man, I realize this as well. By offering you my assistance, I am helping to insure my safety as well as that of my family."

Steve considered and slowly began to smile.

"You are a smart man. When you get out, I might want you to come work for me. I have many uses for a man of your talents. One thing bothers me about this situation though."

"What is that?"

"You are in here. Everyone and everything having to do with the artificial retina project is out there. Regardless of any

125

ingenious plan that you may devise, how are you going to influence it in any way?"

"I will need someone on the inside to actually execute the plan but I think that I already have that covered."

"Really? Who do you have in mind?"

James considered whether it was wise to say anything about Ben to Steve. He decided that Steve would have to know eventually anyway and so he may as well go ahead and tell him.

"I think that we can use Ben Nelson."

"Ben?"

"Yes, Ben. He is already working for Vision Biotech and I suspect that he would be open to making some money."

Steve's expression changed. James could not read it and that worried him.

"Actually, I already know that Ben is working for Vision Biotech. It is my business to know such things. What I wonder is how you know it and how you know of his financial interests."

James' heart rate quickened. He had been careless and he needed to recover quickly.

"I worked in the biotech industry for a long time. I hear things. Even in here, we get newspapers and other periodicals. Beth tells me things too."

Steve seemed satisfied and James heart rate slowed.

"OK. I will be back in a week. By then, make preparations to get me the computer. When we next meet, tell me how to get it and be ready to give me a rough outline of what you have in mind."

"OK. Will do."

Steve had been all business, just as in their previous meetings. Just as he went to summon the guard so he could leave, Steve quickly turned back. His expression was neutral but, when he spoke, his voice conveyed an ominous tone.

"James, never double cross me. I will always be fair with you. If you do what you say, I will repay you. If you do not, I will repay that as well."

Chapter 29

Christine watched Brother Luke step behind the pulpit. She wondered what message he would have to bring to his flock this Easter. She prayed that it would be something relevant to both her and to Dan, whom she had finally gotten to attend a service. Though she was making slow progress, she still struggled with coming to peace with her past with Roger. Although he hadn't directly said anything about it, she sensed that Dan was struggling with his relationship with God or, to be more accurate, his lack of a relationship and whether he wanted there to be one. She couldn't imagine how a single sermon could address both of these very different issues but she had certainly seen God do more miraculous things and so, with an open heart and an expectant spirit, she waited.

"One of the most amazing things about what Christ did for us on the cross is the love for us that he demonstrated. Think about it. He never did anything wrong but He was executed by the most horrific method ever devised. He was God incarnate. As He Himself said, He could have stopped it at any time. Yet, he loved us so much that he endured it, willingly, in order to pay for our sins. This is the greatest example of love in history. As Christians, we are to demonstrate this same love."

Christine glanced over at Dan. It looked as though he was listening intently. She smiled. She was very glad to see that he appeared to be receptive.

"Christ died on the cross so that our sins might be forgiven. He even openly forgave those who had just crucified Him. One of the ways that we demonstrate this same love to others is by forgiving them in the same way that Christ has forgiven us. This morning, I want to talk to you about that."

Christine thought "Oh boy, I wanted something relevant and I sure got it". She was a little apprehensive that she was probably about to get her toes stepped on but she was more excited to see the spiritual truth that God would illuminate for her through the words of Brother Luke.

"Forgiveness. Easy to say. Very hard to do."

Christine thought "Tell me about it".

"The bible says, in Mark 12:31, 'You shall love your neighbor as yourself'. This can be the hardest commandment to keep but doing so is absolutely vital to your fellowship with God. There are several reasons for this and there is a whole lot to say about it. I will talk more about this in other sermons but, today, I will focus on only one aspect. That is, in order to truly receive God's forgiveness and walk in fellowship with Him, we must sincerely forgive others."

Christine thought "Here comes the toe stomping".

"The Bible says, in 1 John 4:20, that we cannot hate one another and yet love God. Matthew 6:14-15 says that if you forgive men their trespasses then your heavenly Father will also forgive you but if you do not forgive men their trespasses then neither will your Father forgive your trespasses. Hmmm, kind of harsh, isn't it, God? I mean, seriously, there are things that don't deserve to be forgiven, right? So why does the Bible say that? I use to wonder about that."

Christine thought "I still do wonder about that".

"I think that it is instructive to back up a couple of verses, to verse 12, which asks God to forgive us our debts as we forgive our debtors. Do we really want God to do that? This verse implies that our debts will only be forgiven if we forgive those who owe us. At first glance, this seems a bit harsh as well but, if we really think about it, it has to be this way and this verse will help us to understand why."

Christine didn't feel as though she was getting much spiritual illumination and she hoped that Brother Luke would get into the meat of it shortly. She didn't have to wait long.

"Think about something. Christ paid our sin debt, a debt which we could not pay. He also paid the sin debt of our enemies. He satisfied all debts, in full, and He did so using the same currency, His righteousness, a currency which we do not possess. We cannot very well demand payment for a debt that has already been paid. If we say that the currency was no good to pay that debt, then it must have also been no good to pay our debt which then, apparently, remains unpaid as well. He paid or He didn't. We can't have it both ways."

Hmmm. That did make a lot of sense but Christine had never thought about it in that way before. She glanced over at Dan, who appeared to still be listening intently.

"Think about it this way. Let's say that I have gone to lunch with Mike, my brother, and Jerry, our youth pastor here. Some of you may remember that I wrote a small devotional book a few years ago. Just before we go into the restaurant, Jerry tells me that he wants one of my books. I tell him that they are $10 and he says that's fine. I give Jerry the book and He tells me that he will pay me later. We enjoy our meal and time of fellowship. When the waiter brings the check, it is for $40. Mike, being generous, lays down two twenties and a ten, and says that this will cover the meal and the book. I ask what he is talking about. He says that he has really enjoyed our time of food and fellowship and he wants to cover our meals and, also, being a good church member, he also wants to pay for some spiritual insight from a premier Christian author for our youth pastor so he wants to pay for the book that I previously gave to Jerry. Now wait a second. I tell Mike that I wrote the book and I want to get paid for it. Mike says that payment is indeed deserved and that he is paying the debt. I say that I don't like this. I wrote the book, Jerry will read the book, and I want to get paid by Jerry. I tell Mike that his money is no good for this debt. The waiter breaks in and says to me 'Excuse me sir, I will need some payment for your meal'. I say 'My brother here has generously paid for it'. The waiter says 'But I just heard you tell him that his money is no good to you so it must be counterfeit and you must pay me yourself'."

Now, Christine was getting some spiritual illumination and it was from a spiritual spotlight, shined by God Himself, from which all true spiritual illumination comes. In Brother Luke's hypothetical story, she was like Luke, wanting payment, Roger was like Jerry, owing a debt, and Mike was like Jesus, offering to pay that debt.

"All of the time, people do things that they can't make up for, even if they wanted to, which often they don't. How does a drunk driver bring back a dead child? How does a cheating spouse bring back trust to a marriage? How does an abusive parent undo past pain that they have inflicted? They can't. They may or may not be remorseful but, regardless, they owe a debt that they can't pay. No matter how much we deserve payment, they can't pay us because they don't have the proper currency."

Though she had never thought about it in quite that way, it did feel to Christine as though she was waiting for Roger to make things right with her and it angered her that he didn't. But how could he? He couldn't undo the hurt that he had caused her. He had hurt her, badly, and he did owe her, big time, but he didn't have the means to pay her. Even if he wanted to, he really couldn't set things right.

"We may not have done whatever they did to us but we are sinful too and, in God's eyes, our sin is just as bad. Romans 3:10 says that no one is righteous and Romans 3:23 says that all have sinned and come short of the glory of God. Read Romans 6:23. The first part says 'the wages of sin is death'. That is what we owe God for our sin. What does the next part of Romans 6:23 say? It says 'but the gift of God is eternal life through Jesus Christ our Lord'. Eternal life is a gift. It is not and cannot be earned. How did Jesus pay for this gift? 2 Corinthians 5:21 says that Christ never sinned but he took our sins on himself and Romans 5:8 says that He died as punishment for those sins. So, the son of God paid for the most precious gift that we could ever receive with his own blood. That blood covers all our sins, mine, yours, and all our enemies. We had better be careful about saying that it doesn't cover theirs because, if it doesn't, then it must not cover ours either and, in light of the fact that we have no currency (see Romans 3:10), where does that leave us?"

Good question. Christine had been saved at the age of 11. She had owed a sin debt that she could not pay and so she had trusted in Christ to cover that sin debt with His own righteousness and His own blood. In not forgiving Roger, in not allowing Christ's blood to cover Roger's sin debt against her, she was sinning against God. Was this sin causing a separation between her and God, not allowing her to fully seek His power to heal old wounds and revitalize her and Dan's relationship?

"I have struggled with hatred. I won't go into the reasons here but, for a period of time until about a year ago, I hated someone for what they had done to someone very close to me and, from a worldly prospective, I was absolutely justified. Until I let go of the hatred, this destroyed my fellowship with God but I didn't realize it until God had taken the hatred from me. And He did take the hatred from me because I, myself, could not let go of it. I tried. Well, I sort of tried. Deep down, I didn't want to let go of it. I knew that this hatred was a sin and that it caused Jesus to bear a great deal more suffering on my behalf. Still, I could not or would not let go of it. I came to a point where I had to ask God to forgive me for everything that I had put Him through as a result of this hatred and, broken before Him, I finally sincerely asked him to take it from me. He did. The moment that God took that hatred from me is the moment that my relationship with Him started to heal."

Christine thought back to what Brother Luke had told her about his struggle to forgive the drunk driver who had caused the paralysis of Blake, his son.

"If you are harboring hatred in your heart, you must get rid of it. If you can't, you must ask God to take it. If you sincerely ask, He will take it. You may be completely justified in feeling the way that you feel. I certainly was. But I'm telling you that you cannot feel that way and enjoy fellowship with God. Until you leave the hatred behind, you will never truly fulfill God's purpose for your life and you will never truly walk in fellowship with Him."

Christine now knew what she had to do and she couldn't wait to spend some time, in her sewing room, on her knees, alone with God.

Chapter 30

Dan sat in his study, very deep in thought. He had been captivated by the sermon that Brother Luke had preached that morning. Dan was absolutely amazed by the kind of love that Brother Luke had described, the kind of love that Jesus had shown to all of humanity and the love that Christians were supposed to themselves exhibit. He sat and thought about that love. He had to admit that it was a love that he had seen lived out in Christine. He also had to admit that it was a love that was humanly impossible. No one could possibly exhibit that kind of love, consistently, without another power working through that person. These things that Christine, David Landers, Mike Hannon, and Brother Luke talked about must be real. Dan wanted that love and that power.

How did he get it? He didn't know. It seemed as though Brother Luke had alluded to it in the sermon but he didn't really come right out and explain it. Dan didn't want to bother Brother Luke on Easter afternoon, when he was probably spending time with his family. Dan felt sure that Christine could help him but she was in her sewing room with the door shut and he had heard her voice earlier. She was probably on the phone. Of course, he could just wait a little while but, strangely enough, though a relationship with God was something that he had never given much thought to until very recently, now that he had made his mind up to establish a relationship, he didn't want to wait. He sat and pondered for a few minutes.

Then, it came to him. When he had watched David Landers' Christian testimony on YouTube, near the end, David had said something about the plan of salvation, which he said that he had explained in another video on YouTube. Dan had seen it listed but he hadn't clicked on it. He was going to click on it now and he couldn't get his computer booted up fast enough.

Soon, his screen was again filled with the image of David Landers.

"Hello. I am David Landers. If I may, I would like to take a moment to talk with you about the most important thing in my life."

Dan leaned forward and listened, already captivated in anticipation of what was to come.

"I have told you of my challenges. In life, we all face challenges. Everyone has something that makes their life harder than the next person's. For me that something is being blind. For you, I don't know what it is but there is something. Sometimes, as we struggle to face life's challenges, we also struggle to hold on to hope or we lose hope all together. For many people, what hope they do have is tied to the things of this world, things that will not last. But, you know what? You can obtain a hope that is eternal. Not just a hope but an assurance. I have that assurance, in Jesus Christ, who is my Lord and Savior."

Yes, this was what Dan wanted to know about.

"Let me ask you the most important question that anyone can ask you. Do you have the eternal assurance that I have in Jesus Christ? I'm not talking about being a good person or going to church. Is Jesus Christ your Lord and Savior? If He is not or if you really don't know, please keep watching."

Dan thought "Oh, I will keep watching, count on it".

"How are we saved? Can we be good enough? Romans 3:10 says that no one is righteous and Romans 3:23 says that all have sinned and come short of the glory of God. So no, we cannot be good enough because we all sin."

Dan had always considered himself to be a pretty good person but that was in comparing himself to other people, a pretty low standard in some cases. Dan supposed that, when comparing himself to God, he did fall pretty far short of perfection.

136

"What do we deserve because of that sin? Read Romans 6:23. The first part says 'the wages of sin is death'. What are 'wages'? They are what we get for doing something, like getting paid for doing a job. So, what we should get for our sin is death. In this case, what does 'death' mean? Does it mean God should Kill us? No, of course not. It means eternal spiritual separation from God. After physical death, it also means going to Hell. So, for our sin, we deserve to be eternally separated from God and forever burn in Hell."

Dan looked over at the fireplace and thought back to the fires that had burned there before. Briefly, he tried to imagine being in the fire. He couldn't stand the thought of burning at all and certainly not forever.

"So, that's it? No! What does the next part of Romans 6:23 say? It says 'but the gift of God is eternal life through Jesus Christ our Lord'. How did Jesus pay for this gift of eternal life? 2 Corinthians 5:21 says that Christ never sinned but he took our sins on himself and Romans 5:8 says that He died as punishment for those sins. So, the son of God paid for the most precious gift that we could ever receive with his own blood."

He took our punishment? Dan wondered exactly what that might have entailed. Of course, death by crucifixion was horrible in itself. But, for Jesus, was it even more than that? If the deserved punishment for sin was burning in Hell, did Jesus in some way take that on himself too? Dan again looked over at the fireplace and shuttered. Jesus' love really was a love like no other.

"How do we get this gift? Read John 3:16.
For God so loved the world
that he gave his only begotten Son (Jesus)
that whoever believes in him (whoever means everyone)
should not perish, but have everlasting life (not die spiritually and remain forever separated from God but live with Him forever)"

Dan thought "That sounds wonderful but how do I do this". He didn't have to wait long for the answer.

"To get this gift from Jesus, you have to ask him to save you. Romans 10:13 says that 'whoever shall call upon the name of the Lord shall be saved'."

Dan thought "I'm ready to call on His name". He bowed his head as the video continued to play.

"You have to pray and ask Jesus to save you and that goes something like this: 'Jesus, I know that I am a sinner and that I deserve to be separated from God for eternity. I know that I don't deserve forgiveness but you died to save me from my sins. I want you to come into my heart and save me and I give my life to you'."

Dan paused the video. Although David was done with his example prayer, Dan wasn't done with his real prayer. He wanted to tell God everything that he had done wrong that he could think of and he wanted to tell God how sorry he was and how grateful he was that God had sent his Son to take Dan's punishment and to save him. When Dan was finally done, he let the video resume.

"When we are saved, we have to repent, which means to turn from our sins (Acts 3:19). Even Christians still sin but we have to try hard not to and always try to do better."

Dan thought that of course he would try to do better, out of gratitude for Jesus taking his punishment and not wanting to put Him through any more punishment for additional sin.

"We should be baptized after we are saved (Matthew 28:19). Baptism symbolizes his death, burial, and resurrection. This tells the world what we have done."

Yes, baptism, Dan would have to talk to Brother Luke about that. He thought that he got the basic symbolism. He wanted to understand the specifics a little better but, regardless, if it meant being obedient to Jesus, then he wanted to do it.

"Did you pray the prayer above or something similar? If you did and you were sincere then your name is now written in the Lamb's Book of Life. If you have never prayed that prayer, if you do not have a personal relationship with Jesus Christ, then I urge you to give this your full attention. Nothing is more important. In John 14:6, Jesus said 'I am the way, the truth, and the life: no one comes to the Father, except by me'. Do you know him?"

Dan thought "I do now" and a huge smile spread across his face. He couldn't wait to tell Christine.

Chapter 31

Christine sat down in her sewing room, in the same chair where she had knelt to pray two months earlier, just before they had hired Ben. Now, she thought back to that prayer and about how she had felt God talking to her that night. Back then, even as she had prayed and had felt the Holy Spirit communicating with her spirit, she had wondered if God was trying to talk to her about forgiveness and she had thought that He had been. Even though she had been obedient to the Spirit and had asked Dan to hire Ben, she had not really forgiven Ben. She knew that this was not an issue that she could put off any longer.

Now, looking back over the past two months, the situation with Ben did seem to be working out well but, regardless of how it turned out in the end, Christine knew that she had to forgive him. Perhaps Ben was remorseful and perhaps not. Perhaps his motives were pure and perhaps not. Actually, she tended to think not. She was still suspicious of him but that didn't matter. This wasn't really about what or who Ben was. It was about what Jesus was and what He had done for her. He had forgiven her when she did not deserve to be forgiven and when He had known that she would still continue to sin. His blood covered her sins. It covered Ben's as well. As a Christian, she owed Ben the same mercy, the same forgiveness, deserved or not, which Christ had demonstrated toward her.

She thought about this as she turned to a passage that was familiar to her, Romans 5:8. She read "God demonstrates His own love toward us, in that while we were still sinners, Christ died for us". That was a very powerful passage. How many times had she read that passage in various Bible studies and, occasionally, on the shamefully few times when she had walked someone through the plan of salvation. She had heard and read it so many times and, yet, she had not grasped the full meaning of it until now. Even now, really, she knew that she probably hadn't grasped the full meaning. That was one thing that she had learned about scripture. There were volumes of meaning in each verse. She had heard Brother Luke say that the only spiritual truths that were ever truly understood were truths that were taught by the Holy Spirit. The Spirit would illuminate more meaning and allow a person to understand more spiritual truth from scripture, right when they needed it. Now, she thought about the newly illuminated meaning in this verse as it pertained to her own life.

God had sent His own Son, to die for her sin, while she was yet a sinner, continuing to sin. She knew that according to 2 Corinthians 3:18, Christians were to be conformed to His image. This meant that they were to act like Him. Regardless of what Ben had done and even might be continuing to do, Christine had to forgive him, just as Christ had forgiven her while she was yet a sinner.

This wasn't only true of Ben. It was true of Roger as well. Forgiving Roger would be even harder. Because of things that had been set in motion by Ben and because of associations that he had, she had endured some pain. However, though Ben had been one cause of the pain, Ben had not directly inflicted the pain himself. On the other hand, with Roger, there were years of pain, psychological and even some physical, inflicted directly by Roger himself. Ben might not be remorseful. Roger certainly was not remorseful. Still, the same standard applied, the standard of Christ's love, demonstrated toward her which she was then commanded to demonstrate to others. Christine still had a problem. She now clearly understood that, as a Christian, she had to forgive Ben and Roger. For the most part, she even understood why. However, she didn't fully understand how. Still, she now knew, ultimately, that she could do it, in God's love, not her own, because now there was a difference. Really thinking about and better understanding what Christ had done for her made her want to do the same for others, even if she didn't fully understand how to do it, and this truly wanting to was the difference. Before, she knew that hating was not good. She knew that, as a Christian, she was not supposed to hate. Still, deep down, she had not wanted to forgive people like Ben and especially Roger. Not even wanting to forgive, not even wanting to be obedient to Christ was a sin. She knew that sin that a person did not confess to God, that they did not try to deal with before Him, would cause a separation between that person and God and would hamper their communication with Him. The Bible said so in Isaiah 59:2. But now that she actually wanted to be obedient, now that she actually wanted to forgive, she could talk to God about it and He would help her to do what she could never do on her own.

She began to pray. She told God that she was thankful for Him sending Jesus to die for her sins while she was yet a sinner. She was thankful that Jesus had been obedient to the Father, even to the death of the cross, in order to carry out the Father's plan. She told Him that she wanted to demonstrate that same obedience and, in so doing, demonstrate that same love. She was honest with God. She told Him that there were things that she didn't know how to forgive, especially in Roger's case, but she wanted to forgive if God would just show her the way and help her. As she prayed, she also wept, and she knew God felt her pain and her tears brought Him great sorrow. At the same time, she knew her desire to be obedient brought Him great joy and, because she truly desired to be obedient, He would help her to be obedient. She knew, through Him, though it would still not be easy, she could now do what she had failed to do on her own. She was grateful to have someone to help her to bear this load, someone who actually could bear it without it crushing them, as it had her. Though she knew there would still be difficult times ahead, a wonderful peace spread over her.

Just as she finished, there was a knock on the door. She said "yes" and before that one syllable was out of her mouth, the door burst open. There stood Dan, looking happier than she ever remembered seeing him. He said "Boy have I got something to tell you".

Chapter 32

At 8:00 on Monday morning, Ben sat at his desk, staring at his to do list for the day, which was quite long. Dan had just called and said that he wouldn't be in to the office until at least mid-morning because he and Christine had to go to their church to talk to the pastor. Ben found this a bit puzzling because he had never thought of Dan as a religious man. He didn't dwell on it though because it was of no consequence to him. Jake was riding with Dan to and from work, until he got his own driver's license, and so Jake also wouldn't be in until later. Ben was glad that he would have the office to himself for a couple hours.

Ben was surprised by the sudden opening of the front door. In walked a man that Ben was certain that he had never seen and so he assumed that he was there to see Dan or Jake.

"Good morning. If you are here to see Dan or Jake, they aren't here yet."

"Yes, I know that they aren't here yet and won't be here for a while yet, not until at least mid-morning. That is why I am here now. I want to see you, not them, and I want to talk to you privately."

Ben was surprised and a bit taken aback. This guy had a very take charge attitude, which Ben found a bit disconcerting.

"How do you know that they won't be here until at least mid-morning and why do you need to see me?"

"As to how I know what I know, I have my ways and I know many things, some of them even about you. As to why I want to see you, that will become clear very shortly. By the way, I'm Steve Levett."

As Steve spoke, he sat, uninvited, in one of the chairs across from Ben. As he introduced himself, he extended his hand across the desk to Ben.

Ben did not take it. He was getting angry at Steve and his presumptive attitude.

"Where do you get off, coming in here uninvited like you own the place and with this attitude! You say that you know things about me! What about me could possibly interest you and why is it any of your business anyway!"

Ben was shouting and his face was getting redder with every word, while Steve remained totally calm and unruffled, which irritated Ben even more.

"I do know many things about you. For one thing, you accuse me of coming in here like I own the place, but I know that you did once own this place, not the building but the company. I know of the disgrace that accompanied your fall."

"The whole world knows that."

"Yes, they do, and I'm sure that's quite humiliating, especially for a man who has enjoyed the prestige that you once had in the scientific community. Because of that, I bet you would like a little revenge against those responsible for your fall."

Ben's color was returning to normal.

"Are you talking about the Richardsons or the Patrillos?"

"I am talking about the Richardsons. If it wasn't for them and their snooping, your connection to the Patrillos would never have been uncovered and you would be one of the wealthiest and most powerful men in the country right now. In fact, I'm sure that you already know that and I'm sure that is why you are working here. Some time, you will have to tell me how you managed to pull off getting a job here."

They sat in silence for a few minutes.

"Well, wouldn't you like revenge against the Richardsons? I can't help but notice that you did not deny my accusation that you are here for revenge."

"Sure I would but what does that have to do with you?"

"I may be able to help you with that. I too have a vested interest in them not succeeding."

144

Ben was surprised. He knew of no other enemies that the Richardsons were likely to have, other than perhaps the Patrillos, and this guy didn't look like he would be one of their henchmen. Besides, if the Patrillos wanted to get even with the Richardsons, they certainly wouldn't need Ben to help them do it.

"Why? What have they done to you?"

"Does it really matter, as long as I can help you?"

"No, I suppose not, but how can you help me?"

"I have access to a very extensive network of resources and I am developing a plan to bring the Richardsons down."

"I still don't understand what part I am to play in all this."

"I will need someone on the inside and you are the perfect choice. You are probably as motivated as I am to see them fall, though for different reasons. I don't plan to do anything immediately but I probably will within the next few months and I want to know that I can count on you when the time comes."

Ben pondered for a moment. He had his own plan but he had to admit to himself that it was a bit shaky. If Steve could help to get the Richardsons out of the way, so much the better. In the end, Ben just wanted back at the helm of the company, reaping the benefits of the technology that he had developed, and it didn't really matter how he got there. Bringing the Richardsons down seemed very important to Steve. Ben wished that he understood Steve's motivations but he supposed that it didn't really matter in the end. As Steve did seem so motivated, Ben wondered if he might get something more out of this, other than just the fall of the Richardsons.

"This all sounds very interesting. You are correct that revenge is a very powerful motivator. However, I am not only motivated by revenge. I am also motivated by money. As noble as bringing sight to the blind may be, ultimately, I started this whole thing for the money. I love power and

145

prestige too but, if you have enough money, you can buy power and prestige."

"Yes, of course. I did not expect you to work for free and I have brought you a little advance."

Steve lifted a briefcase that Ben had not previously noticed and placed it on the desk. He slid it across to Ben.

"Go ahead and open it."

The briefcase was relatively small. It didn't have combination locks, just two simple latches. Ben popped the latches and lifted the lid. What he saw made him gasp. There were three vertical columns of one hundred dollar bills, five bills in each column. He was staring at $1,500, just on the surface, and how deep did these stacks of bills go?

Steve appeared to read Ben's mind.

"there are 50 bills in each stack."

Ben's jaw dropped.

"So, there are -"

"That's right, there are 750 bills, $75,000. Think of it as a retainer and just be ready when I come calling. There will be more to come when we have accomplished our objective."

That sealed the deal for Ben. This time, when Steve extended his hand, Ben gladly took it. He had no idea how much that $75,000 would end up costing him.

Chapter 33

On Monday afternoon, James Swanson was told that his attorney had arrived to visit him. James assumed that it was Steve. His real attorney, Mark, had not been to see him in months and wasn't likely to come any time soon. There was simply nothing to be done concerning James' case, nothing but wait for another nine and a half years, a very long time. James hoped that it would be Steve waiting for him, for two reasons. First, the money. Second, and more important, at least from James' prospective, working on this project with Steve would give him something to do other than sit in that cell and rot. James didn't suppose that he would actually get much done today, as Steve would not yet have had opportunity to get James' computer because James had not yet had an opportunity to arrange it, but at least James would have a change from his usual routine. Though he didn't really like Steve, James found himself feeling relatively upbeat as he was marched down the hall toward the metal door of the attorney client meeting room.

When the door was opened, James was not disappointed. Steve was sitting there with a briefcase on the table in front of him. Steve rose and shook James hand and the guard quickly left.

"So, how was the rest of your weekend, after I left you on Saturday?"

"Oh, very busy. There was some horrible food to eat, but it wasn't too bad because they don't give you much of it. Then, I re-read a couple books. When I was bored with that, I took a few naps. My schedule is pretty full but I managed to squeeze you in."

Steve smiled.

"I like that. A sense of humor, even in here."

"No point in being too melancholy. It isn't like I can do anything about my circumstances. Anyway, I am enjoying this unexpected break from my very busy routine. I am a bit puzzled at what we are going to do today. I haven't had a chance to arrange for you to get my computer."

"That's OK my man. I knew that you couldn't do much in here so I was busy enough for both of us."

"Oh? How's that?"

The metal table was too small to need to actually slide the briefcase across to James but Steve spun it to face him.

"Open it."

Puzzled, James popped the latches and opened it. Inside, he was stunned to find his computer.

"Where did you get this?"

"From your house, of course."

"But I didn't make any arrangements with Beth."

"Yes, I know. After thinking about it, I decided that it wasn't necessary for you to do so. It would just slow us down. So, I went ahead and got it."

"What did Beth say? What did you tell her?"

"I didn't tell her anything. I doubt that she even knows it's gone."

"But this computer was kept in a safe in my study."

"Yes, a very impressive one."

"Then how did you -"

"Surely, by now, you realize that I have my ways of getting what I want when I want it."

James nodded. He was both impressed and apprehensive at this demonstration of Steve's ability to get things done. He was no longer enjoying the break from his routine all that much but he had increased his resolve to cooperate with Steve and to accomplish their objective, no matter what it took. He had no doubt that this was exactly what Steve had intended. As Steve had just said, he did in deed have his ways of getting what he wanted.

148

With a sigh of resignation, James took the computer out, opened it up, and turned it on.

"What do you want me to do? I haven't had a chance to come up with a plan in the two days since we last saw each other."

"Oh, I know that, and that's fine. It's hard to make a plan without information. That is one reason that I went ahead and got you the computer, so that you would have access to all your information. So, go ahead, work on your plan. Don't worry about me. I will keep myself occupied."

As James began to work, Steve took out a iPad and busied himself with it. After about an hour of looking at schematics and notes, James spoke.

"What, exactly, do you have in mind here?"

"What do you mean?"

"Well, there are a few ways that we can proceed. There is about to be a second implant recipient. We can do the same thing with him that we tried to do with Jake."

"That didn't work out so well."

"No, it didn't, and there is no guarantee that the same thing wouldn't happen this time. After the implantation procedure is done, various parameters will have to be set, and the computer that interfaces with the implants may detect the tampering, just as it did the first time. Also, this time, it would be much harder to get our hands on the implants before the surgical procedure in order to tamper with them in the first place."

"Doesn't sound like a viable option."

"No, not really."

"So, what are our other options?"

"The other basic option would be to affect the first implants, Jake's implants, in some way. If we can gain electronic access to them, there are various things that we can do."

"Such as?"

"There are two basic options. First, we could cause what would look like a malfunction which would cause the implants to stop working or cause them to harm Jake. This, of course, would make the technology appear to be unreliable and unsafe."

Steve nodded.

"I like it. You said that there are two options. What is the second one?"

"This one is much trickier and would require much thought and some research, but I think I could do it. These implants connect directly to the brain, via the optic nerve. It may be possible to use that connection to the brain to influence Jake's thoughts and actions."

Steve appeared to be deep in thought for a few minutes and, as the minutes passed, he appeared to get very excited.

"So, you are saying that we might be able to make Jake do whatever we want?"

"More or less, yes, but I again caution you that this would be very tricky and it is only theoretical. Nothing like this has ever been done before and it is not what these implants were designed to do."

"But you think that you could do it?"

After a moment's hesitation, James nodded.

"I think so, yes, but it will take a while and it will require a lot of meetings with my attorney."

Steve grinned.

"Well, your attorney can easily fit you into his schedule."

"The last time, I mentioned that we will need a man on the inside. With the plan that we are pursuing, that will be absolutely vital."

"No problem, I have that take care of."

"Really, so fast?"

"Yes, just this morning."

"Wow!"

"I told you, I get what I want and I get things done."

Chapter 34

"What else can I do to convince you?"

Jake sat across the desk from David Landers. Jake was still having a hard time selling David on the merits of having the artificial electronic retina implant procedure done and he was starting to get frustrated.

"It isn't a matter of you convincing me. It's a matter of whether I should do it. That isn't something for you to decide. For that matter, it isn't something for me to decide either."

Then who should decide? The Tooth Fairy?"

David ignored the sarcasm.

"God should decide and I have been seeking His will concerning this."

Jake supposed that it made sense for David to say something like that, given his profession. David made his living in the Christian music industry and so he had to keep up a Christian front, so-to-speak. Jake didn't necessarily doubt David's sincerity. He just wasn't sure how deep all this Christian stuff really was and he suspected that much of the Christian life was relatively superficial, even if the person was truly sincere.

"Oh yes, I understand, after all, you are a Christian musical artist and composer."

"Yes, I do work in the Christian music industry, but that isn't who I am. First and foremost, I am a Christian, period. Jesus Christ is my Lord and Savior and I try to seek him in everything that I do."

Jake wasn't sure what to think or say and so he remained silent. David continued.

"I don't always do as good a job as I should, putting Him first and seeking His will, but I am really trying to do it concerning this. This is a huge decision."

Jake now found his voice.

"I'm sure that it's great being a Christian and having your beliefs to give you comfort but think about it man. Why wouldn't God want this for you? This would be so great. It would bring you so much happiness."

David was silent for a moment.

"Yes, I suppose that it would make me happy. In fact, I'm sure that it would make me very happy. The happiness wouldn't last though or it would at least diminish greatly over time."

Jake hadn't known exactly what David would say but he certainly had not expected that and he didn't know how to respond. He was stunned into silence for a moment. When he did respond, it was with an incredulous tone to his voice.

"How could you possibly know that? This has never been done, accept for one time. I'm the only one who would know, first hand, how this feels."

"Yes, that's true. So, let's talk about your experience."

At that, Jake began to get a bit uneasy, though he wasn't exactly sure why. After all, he had nothing negative to say about having received his sight. It had been awesome. Just wait until he told David about his driving lessons. Still, the slight uneasy feeling persisted.

"You have been where I am. You have been totally blind. You know what it is to struggle to be taken seriously by the world because of your blindness. You know of the employment struggles. You know what it is to feel that people see you as less than you really are because you can't see and because that defines you to them. Certainly not everyone is that way but many are."

Jake nodded and David continued.

"You know what it is to long for the independence that sighted people have, to be able to just get in the car and go where you want to go. You know what it is to talk to someone whom you love and you just wish that you could see their face."

Jake nodded again.

"Well, you are past all those problems now. You can see me sitting here talking to you. You can see the computer sitting in front of you and the screen of your phone. You don't have to use screen reading technology any more. If you haven't yet, I'm sure that you will start driving soon. You can go where you want, when you want. You can get into any profession that you choose. I can't imagine what that would feel like. I'm sure it is very gratifying."

Jake smiled broadly.

"Yes, it is very cool. It's absolutely awesome."

"I'm sure. Now, let me ask you a question. You only received your sight about six months ago, so I'm sure that the newness of it and the initial euphoria hasn't quite warn off yet, but tell me something. Is the experience all that you thought it would be?"

Jake wasn't entirely sure he understood what David was asking.

"I just told you that it is awesome."

"Yes, I'm sure that is awesome and even more than awesome but is it all that you hoped for? Is it still all to you that it was in the beginning?"

Jake pondered this for a moment. When he really thought about it, there were more negative aspects to his having gained his eyesight than he had realized. He thought about the whole reverse engineering issue and the internal conflict which that had caused. It had strained Jake's and Dan's relationship, for a time. Even now, Jake wasn't sure that his relationship with Dan had fully recovered. It wasn't just the reverse engineering issues that had caused Jake to experience internal conflict. Hadn't Jake experienced insecurity when thinking about his own accomplishments as a blind person in comparison with what David had accomplished? And hadn't that continued to nag at him throughout the whole process of trying to get David as a gold patient? Even though Jake could see just fine now, his perceived past lack of accomplishment

153

still bothered him, despite what he might now accomplish in the future. The experience of gaining his sight had not, by any means, been all negative. On the contrary, it really had been awesome but Jake did have to admit that, no, it had not been all that he had thought it would be and at least a little of the luster had begun to fade.

Jake had not spoken at all as he thought about these things and now David spoke.

"I realize that, even if some things about the experience haven't been quite what you thought they would be, you may have a hard time bringing yourself to say that because, after all, you are trying to sell me on the same experience. I will save you the trouble. I know that the experience hasn't been all that you had hoped, simply because nothing in this world is ever what we hope. That's especially true of really big things like this. We build them up in our minds to be more than they really ever can be.

You know, lately, I have been pretty financially successful. That hasn't proven to be all that I thought it would be. Now, don't get me wrong. There is nothing at all wrong with having a lot of money and it is pretty cool never having to worry about making the mortgage payment. While the money has solved some problems, it has caused others. Some of my relationships that I thought were rock solid are now faltering because of jealousy. Last year, my 43 year old brother, to whom I was very close, died of cancer. All my millions couldn't stop him from dying and all the pain that his loss caused was not lessoned by not having to worry about a mortgage payment. Nothing that this world offers ever really brings peace, not money, not eyesight, not anything."

Jake was intrigued. David was right. As awesome as being able to see was, it had not brought Jake peace.

"And yet, you seem to be at peace."

"Yes, I am, and I hope to talk to you a bit more about that later. For now -"

David slid an envelope across the desk to Jake. When Jake opened it, he found a cashier's check, made out to Vision Biotech, in the amount of seven million dollars. Jake's jaw dropped and when he looked up, David was smiling. "Eyesight won't bring me more peace than I have now but I think I'll see what it's like anyway."

Chapter 35

Christine sat in the office of Midtown Ob/Gyn Specialists. This was her first visit to the clinic. When she had lived in Memphis, she had gone to a doctor there and, since she and Dan had gotten married, six months previously, she hadn't had any reason to go, until now.

"Christine Richardson"

As Christine got up and followed the nurse back to an exam room, she was both excited and nervous. As the nurse took Christine's blood pressure and recorded some basic information in her chart, she made small talk. Christine found her to be very friendly but she had a hard time concentrating on the conversation. Very shortly, they got to the issue at hand.

"So, you think that you are pregnant and you want to find out for sure."

Christine nodded and smiled broadly.

"Yes."

"When was your last period?"

"Seven weeks ago. Obviously, I missed the last one. I was going to wait until I missed one more before coming in but I have had some nausea the last couple days."

"I see. Do you already have children?"

"No, this will be my first. At least, I hope that it will be."

Christine suddenly realized just how much she hoped that she was pregnant. She was fairly certain that she was but she had not yet told Dan. She planned to tell him that evening if the test was, in fact, positive.

The nurse asked Christine to give a urine sample and then she sat in the exam room and waited for the doctor. It turned out to be a long wait, which gave Christine a lot of time to think. She and Dan had known that they wanted to have children. Both of them had wanted them in their previous marriages, at

157

least initially, but it had never happened. Given the things that had eventually come to light concerning both their former spouses, this had probably been a good thing. Now, Christine and Dan definitely wanted children, together.

They weren't exactly sure about the timing though. Well, Christine wasn't sure. Dan would have loved it if Christine had gotten pregnant the first month that they were married. Christine wanted to wait until she got past her issues with Roger because she wanted her relationship with Dan to be all that it could be so that they could be the best parents that they could be. Now that she was starting to work through those issues, with God's help, the timing could not be better for a pregnancy. She smiled at the thought of how God just always seemed to work out everything.

Just then, the door swung open and the doctor walked in. Christine's heart skipped a beat. The doctor smiled and she knew. She breathed a prayer, "thank You God". She couldn't wait to tell Dan.

That night, Christine prepared a huge dinner, 20 oz. steaks, baked potatoes, big yeast rolls, salads, and two desserts.

During dinner, she and Dan talked about many things, not the least of which was Vision Biotech's recent acquisition of David Landers as their first gold patient.

"It's great and Jake is very excited but, you know, he isn't quite as excited as I thought that he would be."

"Does he seem down about something?"

"No, I wouldn't go that far. He isn't down, really. He isn't quite himself though."

"Maybe he still feels bad about the whole reverse engineering thing."

"That could be. I don't think so though."

"Well, you know, you seemed a bit vaguely distracted for the last couple months or so and, as it turned out, it was the conviction of the Holy Spirit. I didn't know that though until you finally told Him Yes."

158

Dan smiled.

"That's true. Jake and David did spend a lot of time talking when David gave him the check. Maybe David said something to Jake that got him thinking. Maybe the Spirit is starting to work on him too."

Christine smiled.

"I hope so."

"Me too. Hey, I think I'm going to make some coffee. You want some?"

"No, better not. In my condition, I need to minimize my caffeine intake."

"What condition is that?"

Dan was at the coffee pot and, when she didn't answer him, he turned around to look at her. He saw the huge smile spread across her face and she didn't have to say a word. He knew and he was so excited.

"Sit down."

"I am sitting down."

"Then lay down."

She laughed and put her arms around him. They just stood there for a while, holding each other.

When he could speak, Dan said "How could life get any better than this".

Chapter 36

"This is so cool. I can't believe that I am about to see as well as my wife and kids. Heck, I might even see better than them."

"That's true, you very possibly could see better than them. My visual acuity is now slightly better than Dan's, my brother."

Jake sat across from Eric Mathews, the second prospective gold patient. Eric was a bestselling novelist who was also completely blind. He required much less convincing than had David Landers. In the past three years, Eric had four books which had all risen to the top five of the New York Times Best Seller List. Two of those had reached number one. Eric had no problem coming up with the seven million dollars and he had no qualms at all about parting with it. For the second time in as many weeks, Jake had just been handed a cashier's check in the amount of seven million dollars.

Jake was struck by how much easier this was than it had been with David and, as he listened to Eric, he marveled at the difference between the attitudes of the two men.

"This is going to change everything for me, I mean everything. For the first time, I will be able to drive. No more waiting for people to take me places. I will be able to actually see my wife and kids for the first time ever. No more of people saying 'you are going to do what, how are you going to do that, you can't see'. If my writing career ever loses steam or if I just want to do something else, I will have all sorts of options. I tell you, Jake, this is going to be life changing."

Jake had no doubt that it would be life changing for Eric. It certainly had been for Jake. Eric's words helped to reinforce Jake's own excitement concerning gaining his vision. Being blind wasn't as bad as many people might think but it wasn't exactly a picnic either and this technology would change the lives of thousands in ways that they couldn't even imagine. Jake couldn't really blame himself for not wanting to do anything that could possibly result in him losing the newly acquired gift of his own sight. What could be more important? Maybe his refusing the reverse engineering procedure hadn't been so awful, though it was a moot point now anyway.

Still, David's words from their last meeting echoed in Jake's mind. After David had given Jake the check, they talked for a few more minutes. When David had stood to leave, he had said something that Jake couldn't completely get out of his head.

"This is very exciting and I'm sure that it will probably work out fine but, if it doesn't for some reason, that's OK. God has always taken care of me and He will continue to do that regardless of whether I can see."

Jake wished that he could have an attitude like that. Not that anyone could blame him for loving his newly found eyesight. He just sort of wished that it didn't mean quite so much to him. He never let himself dwell on this too long and he quickly pushed it out of his head now, as Eric's words penetrated his thoughts.

"What was that again Eric? I let my mind drift there for a second."

"I said when can we do the surgery?"

"Oh, it will be a while yet. Of course, David is first on the schedule. It looks like we will be doing his procedure in about six months, around October. We should be able to do yours within a month or so after that."

"Sounds good. Farther away than I would like, of course, but I should be able to see the Christmas tree this year. That's good enough for me."

They talked for just a little while longer and Eric left. Then, Jake headed to Dan's office.

"Tell me how awesome I am."

"Oh, you got Eric on board?"

"I sure did."

Jake handed Dan the check.

"Very cool. Now, go get more of these. I've already spent a couple million of the last check you got. With our overhead, these seven million dollar checks don't go as far as you might think."

Both men laughed and then they remained in silence for a few minutes while Dan looked through a stack of documents and Jake just sat there. Eventually, Dan spoke.

"Something on your mind?"

"Oh, just thinking about the difference between Eric and David."

"Oh really? I met both of them only briefly. Is there a big difference between them?"

Dan spoke passively, as though the answer was of no real interest to him, but his expression somehow suggested otherwise.

"Yes. They are both very excited, of course, but it seems like it is a much bigger deal to Eric than to David."

"Oh?"

"Sure seems that way."

"Why do you suppose that is?"

"I'm not sure but I'm trying to figure it out."

Dan stopped for a moment while thumbing through the papers in front of him, as though he was pausing for a moment to think.

"I believe that David is a Christian. Do you know if that is true of Eric?"

Jake had feared this. He knew that Dan had recently become a Christian. Ever since then, he had tended to spiritualize things, to try to run everything through what Jake had come to think of as his Jesus filter. What would Jesus think about this? What would Jesus do in this situation? Maybe I should pray and ask Jesus about this. Jesus this and Jesus that. Jake had nothing in particular against organized religion, including Christianity, though he didn't really feel that it was for him.

163

All of this recent spirituality from Dan had begun to irritate Jake. Dan had apparently sensed this and he had backed off of it somewhat around Jake. Jake noticed a bit of trepidation on Dan's face now.

Jake had two thoughts concerning this.

First, he thought that it was very cool that he could see the look on Dan's face. There had been no note of trepidation in Dan's voice and so, if Jake had not been able to see Dan's facial expression, he would not have known how Dan apparently felt about posing this question to Jake. There was just so much that Jake had missed out on as a blind man and he hadn't even always realized it.

Second, Jake felt bad because he felt that Dan certainly had the right to his new found spirituality and Jake didn't want to be a wet blanket. So, Jake tried to appear relatively neutral in his response, showing no emotion and certainly no irritation.

"I don't know if Eric is a Christian or not. I don't believe that I have ever heard him say anything about it."

Dan continued to look at his documents and again spoke rather passively.

"Well, it's something to think about."

Something to think about? What was something to think about? Whether Eric was a Christian like David? Whether that might account for the difference in attitude? Jake wasn't sure if that was what Dan meant and he wasn't anxious to find out. Jake didn't begrudge Dan his Christianity but he didn't really want to get into a long discussion about it either. Jake quickly excused himself and went back to his office.

Chapter 37

Over the course of the next six months, things went very well for Vision Biotech.

They had managed to get all the capital that they needed. There was the seven million dollars from David Landers and seven million from Eric Mathews. Despite attempts to get others, David and Eric turned out to be the only gold patients. There just weren't that many blind people who were wealthy enough to write a multimillion dollar check. They took the 14 million from the gold patients and then borrowed another 14 million. Dan sold most of his commercial real estate investment property in Atlanta and contributed an additional two million. So, in total, Vision Biotech had come up with 30 million dollars with which to get started.

The majority of this money had been spent getting Biotronics equipped for the production of the artificial retinal implants. About 25 million went into that. Then, Dan had purchased the building which Vision Biotech had been renting and he expanded it, adding an ophthalmological exam room and several offices, plus research lab facilities. Three million dollars went into all of that. Now, 28 of the 30 million of capital had been spent but they were in the home stretch and everyone felt that the remaining two million would be enough to get them through the upcoming implantation procedures. After that, it was felt that people would be clambering to have the procedure done and there would be virtually no limit to revenue and other sources of funding.

There was a whole lot of work that went into getting ready to perform the procedures and Ben proved to be instrumental in this process. They had hired Mark Fleming, an ophthalmologist, and Rebecca Crowder, a neurologist, both of which had worked for Vision Biotech before the scandal which took it down and both of which were very knowledgeable concerning the implants and the procedure. They also had the staff of Biotronics, who had manufactured Jake's implants. Their staff was also very knowledgeable but their staff no longer included James Swanson. As Biotronics head lab tech during the time when Jake's implants had been created, James probably knew more about the technology than anyone, except for perhaps Ben himself. As James was sitting in jail for the sabotage attempt, Ben had to take care of many problems that came up, which he did, very efficiently and very competently. In doing so, he proved himself to the Richardsons and their remaining doubts concerning him seemed to be vanishing.

Ben now sat in his new office, thinking about the previous six months. His good fortune had seemed to start with that visit from Steve Levett. There had been infrequent contact with Steve in the previous six months. Steve just periodically checked in, just to make sure that Ben would still be on board when the time came and, in order to help to insure that, Steve had given Ben two additional payments, though neither of them as large as the first. Steve had not given Ben any clue as to what his plan was and Ben had no idea that Steve was also working with James. because Ben was almost entirely being kept in the dark by Steve, Ben did not yet realize that Steve's ultimate objective was not to bring down the Richardsons, specifically, but rather to bring down the technology that they were working to make available. Had Ben realized this, he would not have been so anxious to work with Steve. After all, Ben's ultimate goal was to reap the financial and social benefits of the technology himself, after getting the Richardsons out of the way. For now, Ben remained blissfully ignorant.

Ben was amazed at how quickly the company had gone through capital. They had spent 28 million dollars in six months. Back when Ben was running the company and initially developing the technology, the capital burn rate hadn't been nearly that high. It had been high enough though. Ben had gone through several million dollars in grants and then, when the grants had run out, he had ended up borrowing almost five million dollars from the Patrillos, a debt which he had been unable to repay. He was very glad that Vinnie Patrillo was currently sitting in jail and unable to reach him. Of course, the Patrillo organization still existed but, from what Ben had heard, the Patrillos were quickly going downhill, now that Vinnie was out of the picture, and Ben doubted that they posed much of a threat to him. In this situation too, there were things of which Ben was blissfully unaware.

All of this blissful ignorance would end soon enough but, for now, Ben sat there, very content at the way that everything seemed to be going for him. He thought about what a huge stroke of luck it had been that Steve had come into the picture. Ben had not formulated a real plan, other than the plan to get employed by the company. After that, he had just assumed that his close proximity to the project and his knowledge of the technology would present him with an opportunity to create an apparent insurmountable problem. The technology would then appear to be unviable and Ben would purchase the company from Dan for a little of nothing, just as Dan had done to Ben, and then Ben would correct the problem, which he himself created, and it would again be clear sailing with him again in the driver's seat. With the entrance of Steve, Ben hadn't had to worry about strategizing. He just had to sit and wait for the opportunity which would be presented by Steve. Ben wondered what Steve would come up with. Probably some sort of financial scandal in which Dan would be implicated, forcing him to step down. Ben couldn't imagine what kind of scandal that would be though, as the company was privately owned and Dan had not gotten involved in funding from organized crime, as Ben had. Perhaps it would be some sort of personal scandal which would leave Dan unable to concentrate on the running of the business. Ben couldn't imagine what that would be either though, short of someone getting badly hurt or killed, and surely Steve wasn't that kind of man. After all, this wasn't Vinnie. No matter what Steve's plan was, Ben was confident that The Richardsons would soon be out of his way and he couldn't wait.

Chapter 38

James and Steve again sat in the small attorney client meeting room. They had met dozens of times in the previous six months. They had met so many times that the administration had become suspicious but they couldn't prove anything as they weren't allowed to listen in. Now, Steve sat listening to what James had ultimately come up with.

"These artificial retinal implants connect directly to the brain, via the optic nerve. It is possible to use that connection to the brain to influence Jake's thoughts and actions."

"Yes, yes, you already told me that."

"No, before, I told you that it may be possible. Now, I am telling you that it is possible."

Steve appeared to get excited, a rarity for him.

"So, you have done it?"

"Yes, I have done it."

Steve exclaimed "yes" so loudly that the guard came to check on them.

"So, exactly what will we be able to do? I mean, can we basically upload a set of instructions for Jake to follow?"

"No, nothing quite that sophisticated."

"What then?"

"You, or whoever you choose, will be able to basically do two things. First, you will be able to control the functions for which the implants were designed. In other words, you will be able to control things about how images are delivered to Jake's brain. If done right, there may be some coercive value in that."

"I see. What else?"

"This is the really good part. You will be able to initiate a signal from the implants to the brain that will render Jake extremely receptive to suggestion. The receptiveness to suggestion will last only as long as the signal is being generated. When the signal is discontinued, Jake will appear to be completely normal and he will be completely normal accept that he will feel a strong compulsion to do whatever was suggested. While it is present, the signal also blocks formation of long term memory so he will not remember anyone telling him to do these things."

"Wait. If I am understanding you correctly then this is the greatest thing since sliced bread but I am having a hard time believing it so I must misunderstand something. Give me an example."

James smiled.

"You could begin to generate this signal from the implants, tell Jake to eat earth worms, and discontinue the signal. He would then go out, digging up earth worms and eating them. He might find it strange that earth worms had replaced pizza as his favorite food but he would have no idea why. It may be hard to believe but that is a literal example that is entirely plausible. I am not exaggerating."

For several minutes, Steve was completely speechless, an absolute first for him. When he finally did speak, his voice contained a note of excitement that it had never before contained, at least not since he had been a small child.

"This is fantastic. We can certainly use this to accomplish our objective. It's too bad that everyone doesn't have these implants. We could basically control the world."

Steve went on for several minutes, congratulating James and talking about other possibilities for what James had developed.

"Heck, maybe I should let the project go forward and even find reasons to put these implants into people who aren't blind."

Eventually Steve came down a bit from his initial euphoria and got down to dealing with practical matters.

"OK, so how do we do this? How do we control it?"

"Did you get the device that I asked for?"

"Yes, I did, and it was very expensive."

"I told you that it would be but it will be worth it."

Steve handed James an object. It was about the size of a iPhone, but a bit thicker, solid white, with a little blinking green light on one end. James took it and connected it to his computer with a cable. After a few minutes, he handed it back to Steve.

"It's ready."

"OK, what do I do with it?"

"You interface with it and control it by using your iPhone or a iPad would also work."

Steve took out his iPhone and James demonstrated how to set up and use the device. Steve was absolutely ecstatic.

"I may just have to give you a bonus for this."

"I'll take it."

"Well, I have to run. The implantation procedure is scheduled to happen in just a couple of weeks so there isn't much time. I have got to get things set in motion."

Chapter 39

Steve walked into Ben's office with his usual lack of any type of social courtesy or regard for what Ben might currently be doing. This still irritated Ben but not nearly so much after Ben had realized that Steve usually brought money with him. When Steve reached into his pocket, Ben thought that it was in order to pull out more money. Instead, Steve pulled out an object and placed it on the desk. Ben looked at it curiously. It was unlike anything that he had ever seen before. It was about the size of an iPhone and, at first, Ben thought that it was an iPhone. However, a second look told Ben that it was a bit thicker than an iPhone. It also had no screen. It was solid white, with a little blinking green light on one end. Ben wondered what in the world this thing on his desk was and he wondered why in the world Steve had brought it to him.

"What is this?"

"That is the key to executing our plan."

"That clears it right up. Now that you mention it, what is our plan? You know, we are quickly running out of time."

"Yes, I know that and that is why I am here. Now, watch and listen and learn."

Steve told Ben what the device could do and demonstrated its operation. Ben was totally amazed.

"We had better not let word of this get out. If people find out that something like this can be done through the implants, no one will want them."

"Well, that would be great, actually, but no one will find out." It would be great for no one to want the implants? Ben was suddenly very puzzled.

Just then, Jake walked in with a steaming cup of coffee in his hand and Steve spoke.

"That smells good. Where can I get some of that?"

"In the kitchen right down the hall."

"Is there cream?"

"I'm not sure. I hate cream in coffee."

Just before Steve spoke again, Ben saw him place his finger on an icon on the screen of his iPhone and hold it there.

"You love cream in coffee."

Steve removed his finger from the icon.

"You know, now that you mention it, I wonder if there is any cream. I have never liked cream in coffee but, for some reason, I suddenly want some."

As Jake spoke, he turned to head for the kitchen and the door closed on his last word.

Both Steve's and Ben's jaw dropped.

"That's so awesome! James had explained it all to me but, of course, I didn't see it actually work until now."

"I admit that's one of the most amazing things that I have ever seen but I still don't really understand how this is going to help us to bring down the Richardsons. What is the actual plan?"

"Well, first of all, you must understand that it is not really the Richardsons that I am after, though they will take quite a bit of collateral damage when the company goes down, and that should satisfy your desire for revenge. Ultimately, it is the company or, really, the company's technology that I am after. That is what I must destroy."

Steve continued to talk but Ben was only half listening. Steve wanted to destroy the artificial retinal implant technology, the technology that Ben had worked so hard to develop, the technology that he had counted on being the ticket to everything that he had ever wanted? Ben had thought that Steve was the key to everything but, really, Steve wanted to destroy everything. How could this be? How should Ben handle it? Briefly, he thought of simply telling Steve that he wouldn't do it, that he wouldn't go along with Steve's plan. That thought was short lived, however. Ben had taken a great deal of Steve's money and he had spent most of it so he couldn't just give it back. Even if he could have given it back, that probably wouldn't have made much difference to Steve. With the resources that Steve apparently had, he was not a man to be trifled with and he no doubt thought that he owned Ben. When it came down to it, he did own Ben.

Ben suddenly realized that Steve was looking at him expectantly and he didn't know why. He had to get his mind back on track. He could figure out all of this later.

"I'm sorry, Steve. What was that?"

Steve spoke with an exasperated tone to his voice.

"I was telling you what needs to be done within the next week. Were you not listening at all?"

"I guess not. Sorry. I was just thinking about all of the possibilities with this mind control stuff. You know, maybe you should allow the project to go forward and look for ways to exploit all of the mind control possibilities."

"No. One day, I may get back to looking at how this mind control technology might be implemented in other ways. For now though, I am going to use it to end this project. Those who I work for stand to lose too much from the success of the artificial retina technology."

Ben didn't really think that would work but he had to give it a try.

"Now, let's get back to the issue at hand. Are you listening this time?"

"Yes."

"I'm sure that you interact with Jake a lot, on a day to day basis."

"Yes, I do."

"And I'm sure that this is often in private, in your office or his."

"Yes. Dan entirely owns the company but, in practice, it functions much like a partnership, with Dan handling the business side of things and Jake managing the technical side. Really, it is me who mostly manages the technical stuff. With the new office space, as you see, I now have my own private office. Every day, Jake comes to me with something that he wants me to look into or to discuss how to handle a particular problem."

"OK, good, good. As basically the partner in charge of the technology, I assume that Jake can get through all security protocols protecting all project material, both electronic data and physical materials. During one of your meetings, when the opportunity presents itself, initiate the mind control signal and give him these instructions. He is to delete all project data from the server and destroy all back-ups. He is also to have the implants that have just been completed by Biotronics shipped here, ostensively for testing in the labs here."

"They are already here for testing. The implantation procedure is in a week."

"Excellent. Tell him to go into the lab and destroy them."

"OK."

"What about the design data that Biotronics has?"

"Because they do not own the patent on the technology, Dan insisted that they not keep the design data on sight. They access all project data from our servers and all back-ups are kept here."

"Excellent. So, when Jake destroys all electronic data and project materials that are here, he will be destroying everything related to the project."

"That is correct."

Steve smiled broadly.

"This is going to be easier than I thought."

Ben nodded and said "pretty easy", all the while thinking "What in the world am I going to do about this". He thought that at least things couldn't get any worse. He was wrong.

Chapter 40

As soon as Steve left, Ben heard the voice of the secretary come from the phone on his desk.

"There is a Mr. Andreas Dizinno here to see you."

"Does he have an appointment?"

"No sir."

"I'm very busy at the moment. I don't really have time to talk to anyone, especially someone without an appointment."

"I understand sir but Mr. Dizinno is quite insistent. He says that he will take very little of your time."

Ben breathed an exasperated sigh.

"Fine, send him in."

When Andreas Dizinno walked into Ben's office, Ben knew that he had never seen him before. As he extended his hand, Ben took in the diamond rings and finely tailored suit. Whoever this guy was, he apparently had some money.

"Hello. I am Andreas Dizinno, attorney at law. May I sit down? I will only take a few moments of your time."

"Sure, sit down. If you are an attorney, you probably want to see Dan Richardson. He handles most of the company's business affairs."

"No sir. I am sure that it is you whom I need to see. I am not here to discuss Vision Biotech Business."

"What is the nature of the business that you need to discuss?"

"That will very quickly become quite clear to you. You see, I represent Mr. Vincent Patrillo."

Ben's jaw dropped and he became light headed for a moment. Though he was sitting, he reflexively grabbed the desk to steady himself.

"Are you alright sir? You do not look well."

After taking a moment to recover, Ben spoke.

"No, I'm not OK. What in the world does Vinnie Patrillo want with me?"

"Isn't that rather obvious?"

When Ben did not answer, Andreas continued.

"You still owe Mr. Patrillo a rather substantial sum of money, almost five million dollars. That does not include any interest."

If it had included the interest, it would have been 15 million dollars. When Ben had been running Vision Biotech, Vinnie began to squeeze Ben for the money that he owed to the Patrillo Crime Family. Ben did not have it and, in order to entice Vinnie to give him more time, Ben had offered to triple the money. When everything unfolded the way that it did and the company went down, Ben had been unable to pay. He had foolishly hoped that the problem would just go away. Now, the problem was back and sitting right across from him.

"Mr. Patrillo is in a bit of a tight spot just now and so he is willing to let the interest go if you will pay the principal within a week. Mr. Patrillo believes, as do I, that this is a very generous offer."

Ben didn't know what to say to that so he said nothing.

"I can see that you are rendered speechless by Mr. Patrillo's generous offer. This company appears to be doing quite well and you appear to have attained a rather lofty position here. Both Mr. Patrillo and I are quite confident that you will find a way to resolve this debt. I will take your silence as acquiescence and I will return in one week to collect payment.

With that, Andreas stood, nodded to Ben, turned, and left.

Ben placed his head in his hands. What in the world was he going to do? He now found himself as partners in crime with Steve, whose goals were incompatible with his own, yet he could not extricate himself from the relationship. On top of that, he owed Vinnie a five million dollar debt that he could not possibly pay. Ben had started the day on top of the world and he now felt as though he was under it.

The money that he owed to Vinnie was by far the most pressing problem and he turned his full attention to that.

178

How was he going to get five million dollars in one week? There was no question of not getting it. Ben knew what Vinnie did to those who crossed him and he was apparently able to reach out from his jail cell.

Ben thought about the remaining money that Vision Biotech currently had left, about two million dollars. He had no way of getting to it. Only Dan and Jake had direct access to it. Anyway, that was less than half of the money that he needed. Then, he remembered the Richardson Foundation, which Christine had started to raise money for those who could not afford to pay for Vision Biotech's technology. He thought that he remembered Dan saying that she had managed to raise about three million dollars so far. He still had the same problem though. That money did Ben no good if he did not have access to it. What a shame, Vision Biotech's two million and the Richardson Foundation's three million, five million in total, just the amount that Ben needed and he couldn't get to any of it.

Having the needed money just out of reach seemed to make things even worse somehow and Ben began to despair. Then, he saw it. The mind control device, laying on the edge of the desk, where it had been placed when Steve left. Suddenly, Ben knew exactly what he was going to do.

Chapter 41

Christine slowly rolled over and reached out for her iPhone. She looked at the time. It was 6:08 am. That was good. She had slept a full eight hours, which had become very unusual lately. She had been having trouble sleeping since not long after she had gotten pregnant, six months ago. She rolled onto her back and looked up at the ceiling. Actually, she felt pretty good this morning. No morning sickness. Not much pain in her back and hips, which had been a problem lately. She decided to go ahead and get the day started. She rose carefully, so as not to wake Dan, and tiptoed out of the bedroom.

On her way to the kitchen, she stopped by the bathroom. She couldn't pass it without stopping lately. She couldn't pass the nursery without stopping either and she now stood in the door, surveying the room. She and Dan had done it in the last month or so. Actually, she had picked everything out and Dan had done all of the work. He wouldn't let her do anything since getting pregnant, especially as she had approached the third trimester. She looked at the crib and the bedding that it had taken her six weeks to pick out. She looked at the animals on the walls that she herself had drawn and Dan had painted. She looked at the scripture on the wall above the crib. She felt a longing to hold this little life that she hadn't even met yet but who God knew even from before the foundation of the world.

When she got to the kitchen, she started the coffee and poured herself a bowl of cereal. As she ate, she thought about her life and how it had changed in the past year. What a year it had been.

Things had started out a bit rough, partly because of his initial reluctance to get involved in church, but when things had changed in that regard, they really changed. Now, not only did he attend every service but he also got up early every morning to spend time in prayer and bible study. He had even begun frequently helping out around the church and had started talking about perhaps someday teaching a Sunday school or discipleship class. She smiled as she thought back to the Sunday afternoon, six months previously, when he had been so excited that he had almost knocked her down as he literally ran into the room to tell her of his salvation experience. Her reverie was interrupted by the thump of the newspaper against the front door.

She got up and went to the front door, pausing for a moment to place her hand flat on the biometric reader just to the right of the door. In less than a second, she heard a soft beep, which indicated that the intrusion alarm was deactivated for this particular door, followed by the slight clicking sound of the electronic lock being released. This was all part of the very elaborate security system that Dan had installed before they even moved into the house. All this security sometimes made Christine feel like she was living in a prison but she understood that it was necessary.

When she opened the door to get the paper, she noticed what a beautiful morning it was, and she decided to take her coffee and the paper out onto the back deck and sit for a while. She went through the same routine with the security system at the back door and she took the paper to the table and spread it out. She smiled when she saw the front page article, titled "Second Man to Receive Miracle of Sight From Local Biotech Company". David Landers procedure was to occur in about a week.

While she was sitting there, she noticed a small object on the ground, just a few feet away from the deck. It was small and rectangular, about the size of a pack of cigarettes. At first, she thought little of it and she just kept drinking her coffee and reading her paper. Out of the corner of her eye, she occasionally noticed a little flash of light from the object. At first, she thought that it was sunlight glinting off of it. But, no, that couldn't be it because she was staring straight at it now and the light was coming in very regular intervals. And the object was white but was the light green? Yes, it was. This definitely was not reflected sun light. Her curiosity was peeked and she decided to investigate.

She got up and carefully went down the deck steps. She certainly didn't want to fall at this point in her pregnancy. She bent over the object. It was about the size of a iPhone, but a bit thicker, solid white, with a little blinking green light on one end. Suddenly, she heard a noise behind her. Just as she started to straighten up, she felt a crashing blow to the back of her head. She managed to turn as she fell, to avoid falling on her stomach and hurting the baby, she hoped. As she hit the ground, the world swam out of focus for a moment and she thought that she would pass out. When things came back in focus, she wished that she had passed out. She stared up in disbelief at the person standing over her.

"Jake!"

Jake had a strange look on his face that she could not interpret. He didn't look at all angry. He didn't look remorseful either. He just looked sort of blank as he extended his hand toward her.

"Get up please."

Christine gave him her hand and let him help her to her feet. Before she could speak, she heard something behind her. She whirled, which made her a bit dizzy.

"Ben?"

He knelt and picked up the object that had drawn Christine's attention and placed it in his pocket.

"I apparently dropped this. It worked out well though. It drew you out a little way from the house."

"What in the world is going on here? Ben? Jake?"

She looked back and forth between them. Jake said nothing and still had that odd blank look on his face. Ben too had a strange look that she couldn't easily interpret but it wasn't a blank look. It was close to anger but not exactly. It was Ben who spoke.

"You will find out soon enough what this is about. For now, please come with us."

Christine felt a little strange. She didn't know if she had somehow injured herself or the baby when she had fallen. The strange feeling could also have simply been from adrenalin. She was in a panic. What was she going to do? She had to let Dan know that something was wrong. She screamed.

"Dan! Dan! Da-"

Ben quickly clamped his hand over her mouth and placed a gun to the back of her head.

"Not one more sound. Let's go."

They walked out of the gate of the fence which surrounded the house, onto the driveway, and to Jake's truck. Christine wondered how they had gotten the gate open. Even the gates on the fence had biometric hand print readers. Then she remembered. Jake's hand print had been entered into the system. He could have gotten the gate to open just as easily as she or Dan could. What in the world was Jake doing helping Ben? And what did they want with her?

Ben said "Get in the truck".

"This is Jake's truck. You drove Jake? I thought that you didn't have your license yet."

Jake had said nothing since he told her to get up, in the back yard, and she just wanted him to say something. However, he remained silent.

"No, Jake did not drive. I drove. We brought Jake's truck because it is much bigger than my car and I thought that the extra room might come in handy."

Ben roughly pushed her into the back seat and told Jake to sit with her and hold the gun on her while Ben drove. Again, she tried to talk to Jake.

"Jake, you don't have to -"

"I told you to hush!

She knew that surely Jake would not shoot her but, still, the look in Ben's eyes left no room for argument. She thought that Ben just might shoot both her and Jake. She remained silent. In just a few minutes, they pulled up in front of Vision Biotech. She was overcome by a sense of déjà vu as she thought "Oh Lord, please no, not this again".

Chapter 42

Dan awakened and saw early morning sunlight coming in around the edges of the blinds. He looked at the time on his iPhone. It was 6:58 am. Time to get up in just two minutes. He didn't think that he had awakened just because it was time to get up though. He had a vague impression that he had been awakened by something. He thought about that for a minute. It seemed that he had perhaps heard his name being called, a bit faintly, as though from a distance. Had it perhaps been in a dream? Perhaps just his imagination playing tricks on him as he awakened? The 7 am alarm went off. He silenced it and rolled onto his back.

He lay there for several minutes, listening to the silence in the house. Christine was not in bed with him. She had apparently already gotten up but he did not hear her moving around in the house. Perhaps she had already eaten and taken the paper and her coffee out onto the deck. Dan decided that he would go ahead and shower and then go join her.

As Dan showered, he thought about the day and the week ahead. These were exciting times for Vision Biotech. The company was finally about to be able to get back to what it was created to do, bring sight to the blind. Dan felt very blessed to have been given the opportunity to be at the helm of the company. He knew that the company was likely to make a great deal of money in the coming years and he intended to use much of that money to support various types of Christian ministry. He thought it ironic that, in different ways, this technology would bring both physical sight and spiritual sight to many.

After Dan had showered and dressed, he went into the kitchen and got himself a cup of coffee. He wasn't very hungry so he decided to eat light. As he buttered a single piece of toast, he reflected on the fact that he still had not seen or heard any sign of Christine. He placed his cup of coffee and piece of toast on a plate, which he carried to the deck door. As he placed his hand on the biometric palm reader, he began to feel a slight sense of unease.

As soon as he opened the door, what had been a slight sense of unease became much more intense. A quick glance around the deck did not reveal Christine anywhere, though she had obviously been here. The paper and her half empty coffee cup were still on the table.

Dan walked down the deck steps as he scanned the back yard. He saw no sign of her anywhere. He then walked around the house. As he approached the fence gate that led to the driveway, he saw that it was already open. Apparently Christine had come this way. The gate could be opened from the inside by anyone but could be opened from the outside only by using the biometric palm reader so a child playing in the neighborhood could not have opened it. Both vehicles were still in the garage. As Dan continued around the house, still seeing no sign of Christine, his sense of unease steadily grew. With his circuit of the house nearly complete, he paused with his hand on the biometric palm reader for the gate in the fence on the other side of the house. He was now panicked. He was about to enter the back yard but he had already looked there. There were other places in the house that he could and would look but he knew that she wouldn't be their either.

A quick search of the inside of the house confirmed Dan's worst fear. As he collapsed into one of the chairs in Christine's sowing room, he buried his face in his hands. He knew that she was gone but he did not know how, why, or where.

Dan didn't know what to do. Christine's phone had been on the table out on the deck so he couldn't try to call her or track her. He was in despair. He thought "All this security and look how much good it did". That thought gave him an idea. He would look at the security logs, though he wasn't sure what good it would do. He saw that Christine had opened the front door, probably to get the paper. One minute later, she had opened the back door, to go out onto the deck. Five minutes after that, the driveway gate had been opened using Jake's hand print. What?

Just then, Dan's phone rang. He looked at the caller ID. It showed "Vision Biotech".

Chapter 43

Christine sat in the kitchen of Vision Biotech, bound to a chair. Talk about déjà vu. Almost exactly one year earlier, she had found herself in almost exactly the same situation. Back then, she had been held, against her will, at Vision Biotech's facility in Memphis, where the company was then headquartered. It was part of an attempt to silence her and Dan, after they had discovered the connection between Ben and the Patrillo Crime family. In the end, however, the attempt to silence them, along with the discovery of the sabotage attempt on Jake's implants, had ended up bringing down Ben, Vinnie Patrillo, and Vision Biotech, the latter of which Dan was now trying to resurrect. Christine assumed that the fact that Dan was about to succeed where Ben had failed, along with Ben's connection to Vinnie Patrillo, was somehow behind what she was now going through.

When Christine had been in a similar situation previously, Jake had been right in the middle of it with her and, ultimately, he had been largely responsible for rescuing her. It appeared that there was little chance of that now. Jake appeared to be in league with Ben and, though she couldn't imagine why that would be, it certainly appeared as though she would get no help from Jake. For now, it was just her and God. She thought that, really, having only God with her was OK, given that God was the most powerful being in the universe and He loved her like no other could love her. She knew that, most likely, God would eventually enlist someone else to help her too but, in the meantime, she had to figure out what God wanted her to do. She began to pray.

"God. I don't understand the situation that I am in and I am scared. Please protect me. Please protect this innocent little baby that is inside me. Please give me wisdom, Father. Help me to have the discernment to know Your will. Help me to have the courage to do what You would have me to do."

Just then, Ben came in.

"Well, how are we doing in here."

"When you say we, if you mean me and my baby, I am OK, so far, I think. I have no idea how the baby is. I fell pretty hard when Jake hit me. I really should be checked out by a doctor."

Christine didn't think that Ben was likely to show her much sympathy but it couldn't hurt to try and she really did think that she needed to see a doctor because she still didn't feel quite right.

"You look OK to me."

"Looks can be deceiving. Don't you understand that my baby could be hurt, could even die?"

As she spoke, she involuntarily shuttered as a cramp passed through her. Ben definitely noticed but said nothing. Given the way that the conversation had started, he may have thought that this was a ploy on her part to gain his sympathy but it was not and she was worried.

"I'm sure that you wonder why you are here."

"Of course. I also wonder how you got Jake to help you but I'm sure you aren't going to tell me that. For now, though, I really do need to get to a doctor. Just after you came in, I had a cramp."

A look of worry passed over Ben's face and he appeared to consider for a moment. Christine thought that, even for all Ben's faults, he probably wouldn't want to be responsible for something happening to the baby. For a moment, she was hopeful, but then he shook his head.

"No, I don't think so. You may be lying."

"I assure you, I am not".

"Well, let's just see how things go."

Just then, another cramp hit Christine, though not as bad as the first.

"Things aren't going so well."

Ben simply ignored that.

"I want to talk to you about the Richardson Foundation."

"What about it?"

"How much money does it have?"

"So far, we have raised about 3.2 million. Why do you need to know about that?"

"Because I need the money."

"Seriously? My baby could die because of this little stunt of yours and this is just all about money?"

"I think that you are being a little melodramatic about the baby and, when it comes down to it, isn't everything about money?"

"No, everything is not about money."

Ben adopted a mocking tone.

"What is everything about then? I suppose that, being a Christian, you think that everything is all about God."

"Yes, everything is all about God and, now that you mention Him, do you know that Jesus said that it would be better for a person to have a millstone tied around his neck and be thrown into the ocean than to hurt one of His little children?"

"Did Jesus say that? Well, I'm not entirely sure what a millstone is but I'm sure that wouldn't be pleasant. However, if I don't get this money, the fate that Vinnie Patrillo has in store for me may be just as bad."

"Vinnie Patrillo? Great. The Patrillos again."

"Yes, actually, I would agree with that sentiment. However, I don't have time to discuss my entanglement with the Patrillos. I need to get access to that money."

"Well, you are going to need more than just me in order to get it."

Been looked very surprised.

"What are you talking about?"

"Haven't you ever heard of checks and balances? I can't just write a check or go online and make a transfer. The Richardson Foundation has a board. Any withdrawal has to be authorized by the majority."

"Who is on this board?"

"There is myself, Dan, Jake, Nancy Fletcher, and Mike Hannon."

"That shouldn't be a problem. I'm sure that you will cooperate. Jake won't be a problem either. Since I have both of you, Dan will cooperate as well."

"You still have a problem though."

"What is that?"

"There is one other safeguard that I didn't mention. Any expenditure involving more than ten thousand dollars must be approved by at least one board member who is not a Richardson. Do you have some way of influencing either Nancy or Mike?"

A look of anger and extreme frustration came over Ben's face. "No, I don't."

Christine couldn't help but smile.

"I thought not."

After pondering for a moment, with the same angry look still on his face, Ben got up to leave the room. Just as he got up, the worst cramp yet hit Christine and the smile immediately vanished from her face. In tears, she spoke in a pleading tone.

"Ben, please, let me see a doctor. Don't let my baby die."
Ben's face softened somewhat but he did not reply as he left
the room.

Chapter 44

Jake barely moved in time to keep from being knocked down by Ben as he hurriedly left the kitchen. Jake was worried that Ben would wonder what he was doing in the hall outside the kitchen but Ben seemed to barely even notice him as he quickly walked past.

Jake had been listening to Ben's and Christine's conversation. He was very troubled, both by what he had heard and by his own involvement in the whole situation, which he did not at all understand. Jake loved Christine, very much. He had said that she was more like a sister than a sister-in-law and he had meant it. He would never want to harm her and certainly not her baby. He had shivered when Christine had told Ben about what Jesus had said about hurting children. This was a situation that Jake would never want to be involved in and he, in fact, did not want to be involved. So, why was he involved and even helping Ben. He desperately tried to figure that out. Jake remembered Ben having come to his house. He had thought that it was very early for Ben to be there, shortly after 6 am. Jake had just showered and dressed when he had heard the doorbell. Ben had rushed in, saying something about needing to go talk to Christine and wanting Jake to come along with him. Jake wondered why in the world that he and Ben would need to go talk to Christine and especially so early in the morning. Before Jake could say anything, however, Ben took out his iPhone and the next thing that Jake remembered, he and Ben were headed out the door of Jake's house, with Jake intent on helping Ben to subdue Christine and get her to Vision Biotech. Jake remembered going to Dan's and Christine's house, using his handprint to open the gate, and walking around the house with Ben, just so that Ben, who had never been there before, could get the feel of the place. Jake remembered Christine unexpectedly coming out on the deck and he and Ben having to quickly step out of sight so that she wouldn't see them. He remembered, ultimately, helping Ben to subdue Christine and bring her here. And yet, Jake had no idea why he had done these things. It was as though he had gone through everything on autopilot, with no motivation, only intent.

Now, as Jake thought back on these things, he was very confused and he was horrified at his own actions. He was especially horrified at his having hit Christine in the head, causing her to fall. He thought "if something happens to the baby, it will be my fault" and a shutter passed through him as he again thought about what Christine had said about mistreating children. He had to do something, but what?

In an attempt to figure out what he should do, Jake tried to understand what had happened to him to make him act so strangely. He thought back to Ben's arrival at his house that morning. He thought about Ben taking out his iPhone, immediately after coming in the house. Jake felt totally normal and his actions were totally normal, until that point. Exactly at that point, something had happened to Jake, causing him to have a gap in his memory of a few minutes and causing him to have impulses that he did not like or understand but that he could not suppress. What had happened? It had to have something to do with that iPhone. Then, Jake remembered something else. He remembered that strange little white box. The one that Ben had accidently dropped and Christine had come to look at, right before Jake had hit her in the head. Jake was pretty tech savvy but he had never seen anything like that thing before. That little white box must have been involved too, somehow.

Ben's iPhone must have interfaced with that little white box and, in turn, that little white box must have interfaced with something in Jake, something that could influence his mind. Jake's thinking was logical, as it usually was, and, as it took him to the only possible logical conclusion, he had to back against the wall to steady himself. Of course, his artificial retinal implants. That had to be the answer.

Jake was absolutely horrified and sickened at the thought that something that had brought so much good to his life had caused him to perpetrate such evil and, although he wasn't entirely sure how to do it, he knew what he ultimately had to do.

He had to disable his implants. He couldn't simply turn them off or Ben could simply turn them back on. He had to shut them down in such a way that they could not be reactivated. He quickly went to his office before he could encounter Ben again. He knew that he had to hurry. Time was short. Give him a little too much time and Ben would no doubt come up with more irresistible suggestions for Jake to follow. Also, Jake had no idea what might be wrong with Christine and her baby. He had to help her. He had to come up with a plan and execute it, very quickly.

On Jake's computer, he quickly ran the interface program for the artificial retinal implants, the same program that he had used to activate them one year ago. Back then, he had activated them early in order to help to save Christine. Now, ironically, he was going to deactivate them for the very same reason.

Chapter 45

Christine was very scared and very confused. Again, she prayed.

"God. I really don't understand the situation that I am in and I am very scared. Please protect me. These cramps scare me but I know that you formed this little baby and I know that little children are very precious to you. Please protect this innocent little one. Please give me wisdom, discernment, and courage."

Praying made her feel some better but she was still very scared. Had she been wrong to ask that Dan hire Ben? Given the current situation, it would seem so but, no, she still thought that hiring Ben had been God's will, though right now she couldn't imagine why that would be. She also couldn't imagine how and why Jake would be mixed up in all this. She loved Jake. She thought of him as a brother and it hurt her that he had helped to put her in this situation. She was very hurt, scared, and confused. She continued to pray.

She thought about Romans 8:28 and she recited it aloud.

"And we know that all things work together for good to those who love God, to those who are the called according to His purpose"

Despite the situation, she smiled. She thought "Well, God, I love you and I am doing my best to seek your purpose so I am going to trust You on this but I'm still scared".

Then, she thought about 1 Corinthians 13:12 and she quoted it as well.

"now we see in a mirror, dimly, but then face to face. Now I know in part, but then I shall know just as I also am known."

Christine knew that this verse referred to the very limited knowledge of humans as compared to the all-inclusive knowledge of God. In this life, Christine knew that she saw things dimly but, as a Christian, she would one day know things even as God knew her.

This verse reminded Christine of the viewfinder of a camera. Christine had dabbled in photography, as a hobby, and so she knew a little bit about it. She knew that, when she used a very powerful zoom lens, she could see things much more closely but they also looked much dimmer because powerful zoom lenses did not allow in as much light. In contrast, when she used a normal lens, she could see a much bigger field at once and the picture through the viewfinder was much brighter. Similarly, she knew that God, in looking at the big overall picture, could see things much more brightly and clearly than she could, as she was only looking at the things of which she had direct knowledge. God, on the other hand, had direct knowledge of everything and controlled everything, a fact which gave her comfort. She knew that she was always in God's viewfinder.

This brought her back to Romans 8:28. She knew that God had the knowledge and power to fulfill the promise that He had made to her here. Regardless of her situation, God had her right in the center of His viewfinder and, as long as she kept her eyes and thoughts on Him, He would work everything to keep her right in the center of His will for her life and work everything out for her good. She rested in that promise.

Chapter 46

Dan was puzzled. Why would anyone at Vision Biotech be calling him at this hour. No one should even be there yet. He didn't really want to answer it. He didn't have time to deal with routine business right now. On the other hand, it might be Christine. He had to answer.

"Hello."

"Dan, it's Jake."

At first Dan assumed that this was just about routine business and his first impulse was to get off the phone quickly but then he remembered the security logs that he had just looked at.

"Jake, were you at my house this morning?"

"Yes."

So, the security log was correct. Dan was now even more confused.

"Jake, Christine is missing."

"Yes, I know."

"You know? Have you seen her?"

"Yes, I am with her. Well, that is to say that she is here at Vision Biotech."

"Oh good! Then she is safe."

"No, she isn't safe. I'm probably not either."

"What's wrong?"

"I don't have time to explain right now. Just get here fast and approach with caution. Ben is here too and he is behind whatever is going on."

Jake abruptly hung up. Dan tossed his phone on the desk and began to pace. What in the world was going on? Ben was behind this? That made no sense. Sure, Dan had had plenty of apprehension about Ben initially but, in the last several months, he had more than proven himself, or so Dan had thought. Could Vinnie Patrillo have something to do with this? Surely not. After all, Vinnie was sitting in a jail cell. So was James Swanson but they had never caught the person who had hired James. Could this unknown person have now surfaced? Dan knew that he wasn't going to figure out anything or accomplish anything by pacing. He had to get moving.

He flew out the garage door, grabbing his keys from a hook on the wall as he impatiently waited for the palm print scanner. The scanning process took less than a second but it felt like an eternity. Once Dan was in the garage, he was in such a hurry that he clipped his shin on the front bumper of the truck, as he went around to get in, but the pain didn't even register. He jumped in and he hit the garage door opener before he even hit the seat. He jammed his key in the ignition, quickly twisted it, and nothing happened, nothing at all, not even a click.

Dumbfounded, he sat there, with one hand still on the key, while he watched the garage door slowly rise. He turned the key back and forth several times with the same result. He removed the key and reinserted it and tried again. Still nothing. He didn't have time for this! In despair, he laid his head on the steering wheel and tried to calm himself.

"God, I know that you are in control and that you know best but, to be honest, I am having a little trouble trusting you right now. Please help me and Jake and Christine. Most of all, please be with our little baby."

He tried the key once more but the truck still showed no signs of life.

Chapter 47

Jake couldn't imagine what might be keeping Dan. He had not checked the time when he had called Dan so he didn't know how long it had actually been but it seemed like a very long time. It could have actually been a long time or it could have been just Jake's apprehension making it feel that way. He was worried about Christine and he found being blind again for the first time in a year to be somewhat disconcerting. Regardless of how long it had actually been, Jake didn't think that he could wait any longer. He had to try to help Christine himself.

He sat for a moment and thought about the layout of the building. He would have to proceed very quickly and entirely by feel, which required an acute awareness of one's surroundings. Of course, he had done this type of thing for years but not in quite a while now. He found himself wishing that Dan had not had all of the construction done. Before Jake had the procedure that gave him his eyesight, he had traversed the building many times as a blind man. However, that had been before the recent construction had enlarged the building and changed the layout somewhat. Now, he sat, concentrating on the new layout and preparing himself to move quickly and stealthfully, without sight. Finally, he felt that he was ready or, at least, as ready as he was going to get. He got up and proceeded carefully around the desk. When he turned to face the door and reached out for the door knob, he found that he was only off by about six inches or so. Not too bad. Perhaps he was not as out of practice as he had thought. However, once he was out in the hall, things didn't go quite so smoothly. He wasn't bumping into things but, as he moved quickly, with the fingers of his left hand lightly trailing the wall, he always felt as though he was about to run into something, though he knew that there should be nothing in front of him.

He eventually reached what he knew should be Ben's office door, without incident. The door was closed. He listened carefully but heard nothing on the other side of the door, not even the slight rustling of clothing which would indicate subtle movement. Many people had the mistaken impression that the hearing of blind people was superior to that of sighted people, and they often quoted the adage that "If you lose one sense, the other senses become stronger to make up for it". Though this did seem to make sense, there was no medical evidence what so ever to support it. Actually, most blind people just learned to pay closer attention to their hearing, as it was their primary sense, and Jake had learned to pay very close attention to his hearing during his many years of blindness. Right now, his hearing told him that there was no one on the other side of that door. This both encouraged Jake and filled him with apprehension. It was good that Ben apparently wasn't near but, if he wasn't near, then where was he? Just one more thing to worry about.

Jake stepped directly across the hall to the kitchen door. He knew that this was where Christine was being held. Again, he listened. This time, he did hear sound. He could hear Christine softly crying and he occasionally heard words which he could not quite make out but which sounded like praying. After a moment, he heard what he interpreted as a slight gasp of pain. This broke his momentary paralysis and prompted him to quickly enter the room.

As soon as he entered, it occurred to him that this may not have been a smart move. He didn't know where Ben was and, perhaps, he should have listened a bit more to make certain that Ben was not in the kitchen with Christine. However, his guilt over his involvement in the situation combined with her gasp of pain sent him in without much forethought. He heard no exclamation of surprise and felt no crashing blow so he

202

assumed that he and Christine were alone. He had to remind himself that, even when Ben did see him, it would not immediately be apparent that Jake was no longer under his control. Perhaps Jake could use that to his advantage.

Jake had been so intent on his own thoughts that he had almost forgotten that Christine was sitting there and, when she spoke, it startled him.

"Did he send you to check on me?"

"No and keep your voice down because he doesn't know that I am in here."

"Why should he care that you are in here. After all, you do appear to be on his side."

This statement hit Jake like a truck.

"No, I'm not on his side. I know that it does appear to be that way and I don't have time to explain right now but, trust me, I am on your side and I am very sorry for the part that I have played in all of this. Now, we have got to figure out how to get you out of here."

A look of relief crossed Christine's face but it was quickly replaced with a look of pain. This, of course, went unnoticed by Jake but he did not miss the sudden intake of breath, which fed his guilt even more.

"Are you OK?"

"No, I'm not. I think something is wrong with the baby or, at least, I think what is wrong has something to do with the baby."

She paused before continuing.

"Are you OK, Jake? You are looking at me funny. To be more precise, you are not looking directly at me. It reminds me a little of how you sometimes looked at me when you couldn't see."

"Well, there's a good reason for that. I again can't see."

"But what -"

"No time to explain. It's all part of that long story that I mentioned."

"I can't wait to hear it."

Her last word was cut off by another gasp of pain.

"What can I do?"

"You can free me. Then, you could call the police and an ambulance. Do you have your phone?"

Jake slapped himself in the forehead.

"No, I left it in my office. I'll get it. Let me unbind you first though."

Proceeding by feel and with just a little visual assistance from Christine, Jake quickly had her free.

Then, he left to get his phone. He was more confident on his way back to his office as he was again becoming accustomed to moving about without benefit of sight. He quickly got his iPhone and activated Voice Over, Apple's built in screen reading technology. He had used Voice Over for years and he knew that he would have no trouble getting accustomed to it again. However, he decided to wait until he got back to Christine before calling because he didn't want to leave her alone for too long.

As he approached the kitchen door, he heard something that made his heart skip a beat. He heard Ben's voice. It was coming from directly in front of the kitchen door. After listening for a few seconds, Jake was able to discern that Ben was standing just to one side of the door, leaning on the wall, looking in at Christine and talking to her. Ben's back was to Jake and so he had not seen Jake yet. It appeared that Ben had not yet noticed that Christine was no longer bound. Jake knew that even sighted people sometimes tended not to notice little things that were right in front of them but that they didn't expect to see. Right now, he was thankful for this tendency.

Jake tried to remember if there was anything around that could possibly be used as a weapon and he thought back to when he had hit Vinnie Patrillo in the head with a socket wrench in order to save Christine, just one year previous.

With all of the construction that had taken place in the building lately, he wondered if there might be something similar lying around now. He couldn't remember anything like that and he couldn't look around for something because he could no longer look at anything.

As he was thinking about these things, he felt a slight tug on his arm. At first, his blood ran cold. Then, it occurred to him that it must be Dan. The hand that Jake had felt on his arm guided him back to his office. Jake was released. Now that Dan was here, they would come up with a plan, just like they had done the last time, a year ago in Memphis, and everything would work out fine. Jake knew better than to speak here in the hall, where Ben could hear, and so he silently allowed himself to be led. Jake sat down in his office chair and waited for Dan to close the door. Just before the door closed, he heard something that he did not understand. Jake heard Ben's voice, apparently calling down the hall to Dan, but Ben did not call Dan by his name.

Ben said "Steve, what are you doing here".

Chapter 48

Dan pulled the hood release and slammed the door. He went around and looked under the hood. He just stood there staring for a minute before it occurred to him that there was no point in looking. Whatever was wrong, he did not have the means to fix it right then and there. He slammed the hood and leaned against the front of the truck. What was he going to do?

He closed his eyes for a moment and tried to get control of himself. When he opened them, he was looking right at Christine's car. Of course! Why didn't he think of that. Christine was gone but she didn't drive herself. He could just take her car. As he grabbed her keys from the hook beside the door, he marveled at how people don't see solutions that are, literally, right in front of them.

He half expected her car not to start either and, when it did, he breathed an exasperated sigh of relief and a quick prayer of thanks. As he flew out of the driveway and down the street, he made a quick call to Brother Luke. Dan very quickly explained the situation and asked Luke to be in prayer.

"I surely will. I will begin praying now and I will not stop until I hear from you."

Dan mumbled a quick "thanks" and hung up. He then tried to call Jake's cell and then the main line at Vision Biotech but got no answer at either. Just then, he passed the church and thought of Brother Luke continuously praying and he was comforted by the thought, though he was still struggling with entirely trusting God with the situation. He thought about the man who had told Jesus something to the effect of "I believe, now help my nonbelief".

Shortly after that, he pulled into the parking lot of Vision Biotech, where he saw Jake's truck and a vehicle that he did not recognize. He quickly parked and then sat there pondering the situation. He did own a gun but it was back at his house. He hadn't taken the time to get it, a decision for which he now chastised himself. Christine and Jake were in there with Ben and no telling who else. No doubt, they were armed. He quickly looked around the interior of the truck, searching for a possible weapon. He found nothing. Well, nothing to do but go and see what awaited. He got out of the truck and a feeling of increasing dread descended on him as he walked across the parking lot.

As he entered the reception area, everything was as it had been when he had left the previous day. He heard voices coming from the door behind the front desk, which led to the main hallway. As he passed by the desk, he looked for a weapon, but he saw nothing more deadly than a stapler.

As he proceeded into the hallway, he could tell that the voices were coming from Jake's office. He stopped, just inches from the door jamb, and listened.

Chapter 49

Jake was still sitting in his office chair, where Steve had led him, but he now knew that Steve was not Dan. Steve and Ben were sitting across from him and having a conversation that Jake found very confusing.

"Why did you bring Christine here? What does she have to do with halting the project? She doesn't even work on it, does she?"

"No, she doesn't. I needed her for other reasons."

"What other reasons? You should have no other reasons that do not involve accomplishing what I am paying you to accomplish. By the way, is that done?"

"Not exactly."

"Not exactly! What!"

Ben began to stammer.

"Well, I, I needed money."

"Money! Goodness gracious man, I have given you over a hundred thousand dollars so far and that was just a down payment. What kind of money do you need?"

"I need five million."

"For what?"

Jake cut in.

"Excuse me, I hate to interrupt, but could someone tell me what the heck is going on here?"

Steve spoke.

"That's another thing. What is wrong with him?"

"What do you mean? I have complete control of him."

"Well, maybe so, but he can't see. Did something go wrong with the mind control device?"

Ben sounded incredulous.

"What do you mean he can't see. Of course he can see."

"No, he can't. When I first walked in here, I saw him, feeling his way down the hallway. It was very apparent that he couldn't see where he was going. I led him back here and he had no idea who I was until he heard my voice."

"Actually, I still don't know who you are, and please stop talking about me in the third person."

"Jake, shut up. So, Ben, what's wrong with him?"

"I didn't know that anything was wrong with him. The mind control device worked just as expected and I used it to get Jake to help me to abduct Christine."

"Well, thank you for saying that right in front of him. Now, he will have to be eliminated. You have made quite a mess of things for what should have been a very simple job."

Given what Steve had said about eliminating him, Jake wasn't sure whether to say anything. He decided to go ahead. After all, as Steve had just pointed out, Ben had just mentioned what he had done, right in front of Jake, so finding out that Jake had already known wouldn't make much difference.

"Ben, I hear you messing around with something in your hands. If you are playing around with your phone and that little white gizmo, forget it. I figured out what was going on. I permanently deactivated my implants in order to stop you from controlling me. That is why I can't see."

It was Steve who next spoke.

"Well, well, well. What a mess. There is no question that you will have to be eliminated now, Jake, and Ben, you have proven yourself untrustworthy as well. I will deal with Christine in a moment."

Jake heard Ben's sharp intake of breath, followed by the unmistakable sound of a gun being cocked, and his blood seemed to freeze in his veins.

Just then, the window behind Jake exploded inward and Jake felt himself being roughly pushed to the floor. He heard shouted orders to "get down" and the sound of other weapons being cocked. He was then helped to his feet as he heard what he thought was the sound of hand cuffs being closed.

"I can explain."

It was the voice of Ben. Then a voice that Jake did not recognize, which he assumed belonged to a police officer. "You have the right to remain silent".

Then, the voice of Steve.

"I have nothing to say. I will speak only to and through my attorney."

Then the voice of the officer again.

"You are going to need him."

Chapter 50

Jake took Dan's arm and Dan led him into Christine's hospital room. Jake could hear a steady beeping sound, which represented Christine's heartbeat, coming from a machine beside the bed. A different machine was emitting a much faster beeping sound, representing the baby's heartbeat. The sound of the machine keeping up with the baby's heart beat pierced Jake's heart. What had he done to that little innocent life?

As Dan sat Jake down in a chair beside the bed, he heard a nurse's voice.

"I will silence these monitors so you can talk more easily. Don't worry, we can monitor them at the nurses' station."

With that, she left the room and Jake was left alone with Dan, Christine, and the little baby growing inside her. In a way, it was that little baby who was hardest to face. The baby was the one who was in danger as a result of Jake's actions. If anything happened to that little life, Jake could never forgive himself. Even if everything was OK, he didn't know how Christine and Dan could ever forgive him and he would not blame them in the slightest if they never did. No one spoke for several seconds.

Jake asked "What do the doctors say" and, after a slight pause, it was Dan who answered.

"They think that everything will be OK. Christine is fine, with just a couple of scrapes and bruises and a very mild concussion. However, Christine is in early labor and the baby is in some distress."

Tears began to silently run down Jake's face.

"Christine is six months along. At that gestational age, the baby could possibly survive. You know that. You, yourself, were three months premature."

It was Jake's premature birth that had led to his eye condition and he worried that the same could happen to the baby, if the baby even survived. As Dan continued, Jake placed his head in his hands.

"As you know, though a baby who is three months premature certainly can survive outside of the mother's body, they do not always survive and that prematurity can lead to various complications. It is best if Christine does not deliver right now. The doctors are giving Christine some meds to stop her labor. It's too soon to know if it will work but they think that it probably will. We should know shortly."

As Dan had been speaking, Jake could hear Christine praying very softly, though he could not make out her words, and he knew that she was softly crying. His heart was absolutely broken. Jake sunk to his knees beside the bed and he gently felt for her hands and took them in his own. In a shaky voice, he softly spoke to her with tears streaming down his face.

"Christine. I am so sorry. I would have never done what I did willingly. I hope that you know that. I know that it seems like I meant to do it but, please believe me, I didn't. I would never have hurt you or your little baby. I literally had no choice in the matter. I know that you don't understand that. Please let me explain."

Christine interrupted him.

"You don't have to explain. I don't yet know everything but I know enough. I heard you talking to Steve and Ben. I know that they were controlling you, somehow, through your implants. I know that you permanently deactivated them in order to break their control over you."

With tears still streaming down his face, Jake silently nodded.

"That isn't all. Dan has spoken to the doctor who treated you in the ER and so I know that, by overloading the implants, you damaged your optic nerve and so you will probably never see again, even with new implants. You know enough about this technology that I am sure that you knew this would be the result when you overloaded the implants. You will suffer for the rest of your life for your decision and yet you did this willingly, in order to try to help me and the baby."

With tears still streaming and in a shaky voice, Jake spoke. "Yes, what you say is true, but it was still my hands which inflicted the injuries which hurt you and which could yet kill your baby. How can you forgive me for that?"

Jake felt Dan's hands on his shoulders and heard Dan's voice. "The reason that we can forgive you is this. You just made a great sacrifice to try to help to save Christine and our baby. Probably at least part of the reason that you did that was guilt over the role that you had played in placing her and the baby in danger. Nevertheless, we understand the situation that you were in and what you did was very noble. Because of your sacrifice, the baby will probably be fine. Two thousand years ago, someone made a much greater sacrifice than the one that you just made and it is that sacrifice and the love that it represents that allows us to forgive you."

Dan pulled up a chair beside Jake.

"You see, Jake, God is without sin and, in his eyes, everyone should conform to that standard. However, we don't and we can't. We sin against God and against each other all of the time. That is true for both Christians and non-Christians. Because God is completely holy and He is the definition of righteousness, He literally cannot abide sin. So, when sin occurs, it must be paid for. Hebrews 9:22 says that without the shedding of blood there can be no remission of sin. God loves us so much that He did not want us to have to suffer for our sin, so he sent Jesus, the Christ, God's only begotten Son, to shed His blood for our sin. Jesus did this willingly, though He, Himself, never sinned. He had nothing to feel guilty for. This was done not out of guilt, but purely out of love. It is that love, working in and through us, that allows us to forgive you."

215

Jake was speechless. He could not imagine such a love. Over the next two hours, Dan explained many of the things that Dan, himself, had learned over the past several months. When he was finished, he asked Jake if he too would like to experience the same love and resulting peace that Dan and Christine had. Jake said that he would and he knelt right there, beside Christine's bed and, holding Dan's and Christine's hands, he prayed and invited Jesus into his heart. Just then, the doctor came in and told them that it appeared that the meds were working. Christine's labor had stopped and there were no more signs of fetal distress.

"We will want to keep her here for another day or so, just for observation, but I think that everything will be just fine." Immediately, they all prayed again, this time thanking God for sparing the baby.

When they had finished, Christine spoke.

"I am OK. The baby is OK. Jake has found the Lord. All in all, given the circumstances, things could not have gone better."

They all agreed.

Dan spoke next.

"You know, Jake, Jesus will bring you joy. Joy in Christ is the most wonderful thing in the world but it is not the same as happiness. You will not always be happy, especially with the return of your blindness and all of the associated problems. Jesus promised that in the world we will have tribulation." Though they did not yet know it, tribulation like they had never known was about to begin.

Note From The Author

Hello. I am Scott Duck, author of "View Finder". I thank you for reading this book. It is my prayer that you have not only been entertained but have gained something of spiritual significance. I would like to talk to you about that for a moment.

As you were told in the disclaimer at the beginning, this book is a work of fiction. What the disclaimer did not say is that it is not entirely a work of fiction. The characters are made up and none of them really exist. To my knowledge, nothing like the plot of the book has ever actually happened. However, there is one thing in the book that is real.

In Chapters 19 and 27, Dan watches the Christian testimony of David Landers. David is not real. However, his testimony is real. It is my own. I have never had a brother die of cancer and I am not a millionaire but the rest of David's testimony comes directly from my testimony. Jesus Christ is real and what He has done in my life is real. Like David, I am completely blind and I have dealt with a lot of adversity. Much of my life has not been easy. Despite this, I have a joy and a peace that goes beyond the circumstance of my blindness and all my other circumstances.

Guess what? You can have the same joy and peace that I have. It's right there, bought and paid for long ago, and free for the asking. It doesn't matter what your limitations are. It doesn't matter what you have or haven't done. It doesn't matter what you do or don't have. All that matters is that God loves you more than you could possibly imagine with a love that transcends all understanding (see Chapters 29 through 31 and 50). If you have had an awesome life, He loves you. If you have had a life full of heart ache and adversity, He loves you. He wants you to accept His love. Do you want to experience His love? If so, then please read on.

217

I am going to talk about some scripture here. The full text of the scripture follows or, of course, you can look it up in your own bible, if you have one handy.

How are we saved? Can we be good enough? Romans 3:10 says that no one is righteous and Romans 3:23 says that all have sinned and come short of the glory of God. So no, we cannot be good enough because we all sin.

What do we deserve because of that sin? Read Romans 6:23. The first part says "the wages of sin is death". What are "wages"? They are what we get for doing something, like getting paid for doing a job. So, what we should get for our sin is death. In this case, what does "death" mean? Does it mean God should kill us? No, of course not. It means eternal spiritual separation from God. After physical death, it also means going to Hell. So, for our sin, we deserve to be eternally separated from God and forever burn in Hell.

So, that's it? No! What does the next part of Romans 6:23 say? It says "but the gift of God is eternal life through Jesus Christ our Lord". How did Jesus pay for this gift of eternal life? 2 Corinthians 5:21 says that Christ never sinned but he took our sins on himself and Romans 5:8 says that He died as punishment for those sins. So, the Son of God paid for the most precious gift that we could ever receive with his own blood.

How do we get this gift? Read John 3:16.

For God so loved the world

that he gave his only begotten Son (Jesus)

that whoever believes in him (whoever means everyone)

should not perish, but have everlasting life (not die spiritually and be separated from God)

To get this gift from Jesus, you have to ask him to save you. Romans 10:13 says that "whoever shall call upon the name of the Lord shall be saved".

You have to pray and ask Jesus to save you and that goes something like this: Jesus, I know that I am a sinner and that I deserve to be separated from God for eternity. I know that I don't deserve forgiveness but you died to save me from my sins. I want you to come into my heart and save me and I give my life to you.

When we are saved, we have to repent, which means to turn from our sins (Acts 3:19). Even Christians still sin but we have to try hard not to and always try to do better.

We should be baptized after we are saved (Matthew 28:19). Baptism symbolizes his death, burial, and resurrection. This tells the world what we have done.

Did you pray the prayer above or something similar? If you did and you were sincere then your name is now written in the Lamb's Book of Life. If you have never prayed that prayer, if you do not have a personal relationship with Jesus Christ, then I urge you to give this your full attention. Nothing is more important. In John 14:6, Jesus said "I am the way, the truth, and the life: no one comes to the Father, except by me". Do you know him?

The following scripture is from the New King James Bible, Copyright Thomas Nelson 1982.

Romans 3:10
As it is written: "There is none righteous, no, not one;
Romans 3:23
for all have sinned and fall short of the glory of God,
Romans 6:23
For the wages of sin is death, but the gift of God is eternal life in Christ Jesus our Lord.
2 Corinthians 5:21
For He made Him who knew no sin to be sin for us, that we might become the righteousness of God in Him.
Romans 5:8
But God demonstrates His own love toward us, in that while we were still sinners, Christ died for us.

John 3:16

For God so loved the world that He gave His only begotten Son, that whoever believes in Him should not perish but have everlasting life.

Romans 10:13

For "whoever calls on the name of the Lord shall be saved."

Acts 3:19

Repent therefore and be converted, that your sins may be blotted out, so that times of refreshing may come from the presence of the Lord,

Matthew 28:19

Go therefore and make disciples of all the nations, baptizing them in the name of the Father and of the Son and of the Holy Spirit,

John 14:6

Jesus said to him, "I am the way, the truth, and the life. No one comes to the Father except through Me.

Made in the USA
Charleston, SC
11 February 2016